THE
MONARCHS OF
WINGHAVEN

THE MONARCHS OF WINGHAVEN

Naila Moreira

WALKER BOOKS

Copyright © 2024 by Naila Moreira
The worksheet on p. 178 is courtesy of the Monarch Larva Monitoring Project, run jointly by the University of Wisconsin–Madison Arboretum and the Monarch Joint Venture.

First US edition 2024

Library of Congress Catalog Card Number 2023946202
ISBN 978-1-5362-1830-5

24 25 26 27 28 29 APS 10 9 8 7 6 5 4 3 2 1

Printed in Humen, Dongguan, China

This book was typeset in Amasis MT Pro.
The illustrations were done in pen.

Walker Books US
a division of
Candlewick Press
99 Dover Street
Somerville, Massachusetts 02144

www.walkerbooksus.com

To my mother, who made me a writer,
and my father, who made me a bird-watcher

And to Oliver, my sprout

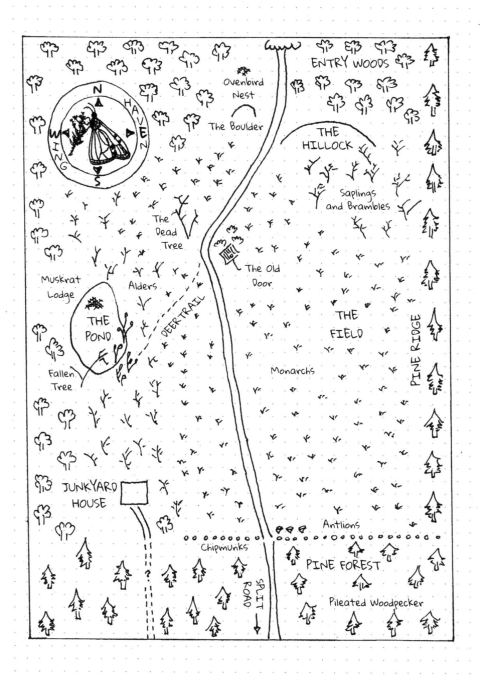

1
THE SECRET

Samantha Tabitha Smith hiked down to one of her favorite spots in her Field.

Beside the path in the middle of the grassland lay an ancient scatter of trash. A broken-down lawn mower. A few unrecognizable scraps of metal. And most importantly, a wooden door.

It lay flat, weeds tall around it. Like she did most days, she wedged her fingers underneath and lifted. The big board parted from the earth.

Jackpot.

On the furrowed soil lay the usual—earthworms, millipedes, pill bugs. But today, better than all those, a rare and beautiful find: a snake skin—and beside it, the snake itself.

Sammie was used to garter snakes. They were slender and dark green with black patterning and long yellow stripes from head to tail tip. She liked to catch them. They didn't bite, usually—or if they tried, their toothless mouths closed so weakly around her finger that she always laughed. But if they twisted and rubbed their scales together, they could produce a nasty-smelling whitish cream that made her fingers smell like she'd dipped them in turpentine. She always held the snakes at the base of their head and the end of their tail, straight out, so they couldn't rub.

But today's snake was different in color and pattern—not a garter snake at all. She'd never seen one like it. It was pale, milky white, with brick-red markings in big ragged patches. It lay curled up and sleeping. She knew it was alive, because its body seemed to glow, shiny and sleek, not dull like the snake she'd once seen crushed by a car.

She didn't touch it. She didn't know if it might bite. Not far off lay the snake skin, coiled, fragile, and transparent. The snake was extra glossy because, she knew, it had just shed its old scales; now it would have space to grow bigger inside its new skin. Reverently, slowly, so as not to disturb the snake, she slid her fingers underneath the old skin and picked it up. It lay like crinkled rice paper in her palm. The whole head, body, and tail were unbroken. A perfect specimen.

She opened her pack and fished out her collecting case, a clear plastic box that wouldn't break but showed the contents, and tucked the skin inside. It followed her personal rule: she could collect only dead things, never anything alive.

Then she pulled out her notebook, a spiral-bound black one with a hard cover. She recorded the date and the weather. She sketched the snake, trying to capture every detail. Sammie had taught herself to draw just for this. She wasn't very good at drawing, but she could at least make a snake look like a snake and a bird look like a bird. Later she would look it up in her field guides at home.

Sammie's teachers always told her she would grow up to be a writer someday. One of her poems hung in a place of honor on the classroom wall. But Sammie liked bugs and birds and snakes and mammals. She wanted to be a scientist. A biologist, to be exact. Yet no one else besides her seemed to care. Science class was so short. The boys all teased her when she asked question after question.

Worse still, Sammie's mother didn't want her to come to the Field alone. The Field was hidden from the rest of the suburb by woodland. It might have been a farm or orchard once, but it had long since been abandoned and returned to nature. Squashed between Sammie's subdivision and the commercial district of Split Road, it was a big swath of wilderness in this busy town.

"It's so isolated and hidden, honey," her mom said. "If anything happens to you, no one will be around to help."

So every day now when Sammie's bus dropped her at

home and her parents were still at work, she came to the Field in secret.

When they'd lived in their old, more rural town, things had been different. Her mom used to pick her up at school in the afternoons, and they would walk together down the street to a conservation area with a little nature center. Sometimes they strolled the paths together, or her mom would retreat with a novel to a big armchair while Sammie explored. Sammie's mom didn't love science the way Sammie did— she mostly thought nature was pretty, like the birds at the feeder she kept just outside the kitchen window. But she'd encouraged Sammie to talk to the staff who worked at Buck Place. "It's important to have a home base in nature, a place to know deeply," one of them told her. "That's how you become a naturalist: someone who understands how all things in nature are connected—from the plants to the animals to the weather and even the dirt."

Sammie had decided then and there that someday she'd become a naturalist, too. Ever since her family had moved here last year, she'd felt comfortable only in her Field. Like the snake, safe under the door while shedding its skin, here she could hide away while she taught herself to be a scientist.

So Sammie had resolved to come here alone. She felt uncomfortable about it, but she pushed the guilt down. If her parents were never around, it seemed only fair to get to make her own decisions. Besides, it wasn't like she was here just to have fun: she was learning new things every day. And she wasn't afraid. If anyone suspicious turned up, she could disappear into the forest like a fawn melting into the underbrush.

And so today, like every day, Sammie had rushed home from the bus stop to her empty house—her parents wouldn't be home from work until dinner. She'd dumped her schoolbag in the garage, strapped on her pack with her notebook and collection box already inside, and hopped on her bicycle to bike the mile to her secret place.

She'd pedaled to the neighborhood's end, her blond hair streaming from under her bicycle helmet as she flew past neighbors' lawns bursting with new grass and daffodils, pretty but tame. Fragrant New England air, warm enough to wear shorts for the first time this spring, washed her legs. After wheeling her bike in a tight circle, she'd dropped it in a hidden place among the bushes. She'd pushed back some branches she'd arranged herself to hike down a short, overgrown path between thick trees. Then the trees opened, and Sammie stood at the top of the Field.

She'd taken a great deep breath and lifted her arms like wings. She was free: of school, mean boys, stressed-out parents, and all the buildings, asphalt, vehicles, and rules that crowded her life.

Almost the only sign of civilization here was this wooden door. Now, still crouched beside it, she carefully closed her collecting box on the snake skin and glanced up through tall grasses waving in the May breeze. All around her she heard birds calling. A common yellowthroat piped a loud *witchety-witchety-witchety-witch!* And then, to her delight, she heard a bird she didn't know. She smiled with excitement. She'd heard the call a few times this spring, but the birds lived so high in the trees at the edge of the meadow, she couldn't spot one. The song rose, a climbing trill of notes like someone running a stick along a musical chain-link fence, welcoming her.

She'd never made a map of this place. Opening to the inside front cover of her notebook, she began to draw again. She sketched the narrow path descending south from the entry woods through a sloping expanse of grassland as big as three or four football fields, patches of shrubbery bunching up among tall grasses. Here where she stood in the very middle, the path turned a slight corner at the wooden door, then continued southward, where it crossed a stone wall into more woods. It took fifteen minutes to hike all the way to busy Split Road beyond. To the west, a shrub-filled decline led down to a pond, then woodland climbed beyond, toward the neighborhoods. To the east rose a steeper hill crested by a long line of pines. The Field was enclosed on all sides.

Only two things interrupted nature in all this space. One

was this scrap heap. The other was a dirt track leading from Split Road to the only nearby house, which Sammie called the Junkyard House. Tucked close to the pine woods and half-hidden down the slope toward the pond, its backyard was a mess, full of rusted equipment and broken-down cars and piles of tires. She could sometimes hear a dog barking wildly, but she'd never seen the people who lived there.

Still, the house was way over in the southwest corner, and Sammie could stay away from it just fine.

This was her kingdom, and it made her powerful.

She finished her map by carefully labeling landmarks she cared about: the Hillock, the Pond, the Dead Tree where hawks liked to land. Then she smiled down at the snake still sleeping peacefully after the hard work of shedding its skin. "You're beautiful, little snake," she mouthed soundlessly so she wouldn't startle it.

With utmost care, she shifted the door from where she'd moved it and placed it back where it belonged, making sure to set it down slowly and exactly as before, so she wouldn't hurt the snake. Then she got up with a sigh of pleasure. She needed to get home before her mom did at five.

She rounded the bend and looked up the slope. Then she stopped.

She wasn't alone.

2

THE BOY

A figure stood at the end of the path, squinting and shading their eyes.

It was a boy.

He was looking at her. Even from this distance, Sammie could see he was about her age. He was wearing ripped jean shorts and a T-shirt, like her. Around his neck hung a black object on a wide strap. *Binoculars?* thought Sammie in surprise.

She considered slipping away into the forest, like she planned if she ever saw a grown-up here. But the boy raised a tentative hand and waved.

Sammie hesitated. Then, slowly, she walked toward him.

As she approached, she could see that he was tall, taller than her, and lanky, with floppy dark brown hair. Unlike Sammie's already sun-browned skin, his complexion was milky pale. Now she could see that the object around his neck was a large camera. She felt a sinking disappointment. Not binoculars after all. She stopped in front of him.

He gazed at her through his tortoiseshell-rimmed glasses.

"Hi," he said.

"Hi," said Sammie.

She wished he'd go away.

"I didn't think anyone else came here," said the boy.

"No one else does come here," said Sammie, clutching her notebook. "Only me."

"That's not true," said the boy. "I come here every day."

"No," explained Sammie with deliberate patience, "*I* come here every day. And you're never here."

She felt glad now that her binoculars were hidden in her pack. Nature watching always got her off on the wrong foot with other kids. Sammie stared hard at the boy, as if daring him to say something unkind.

He looked away first and shrugged.

"What's that?" he said, pointing to her notebook.

She hugged it closer.

"Nothing. Just a notebook."

"What's in it?"

Sammie frowned. "That's private," she said.

There was a silence. To deflect further prying, she added, "Why do you have that big camera?"

The boy seemed to come to life. He lifted it, giving it a

loving look as he turned it carefully in his hands. "This is a Canon Rebel SL-three, one of the best entry-level cameras on the market. It came with an eighteen- to fifty-five-millimeter lens, but I've got a twenty-eight- to three-hundred-millimeter telephoto lens on it most of the time." He twisted the lens, detaching it, then deftly reattached it. The long black cylinder jutted forward like a dog's nose. "I'm a photographer, see?" He touched a button and turned the digital camera's screen to her.

Interested in spite of herself, Sammie leaned forward. A wide-angle view of the Field stretched across the screen, broad and golden. In the distance, a small figure anchored the picture.

"That's me!" she exclaimed with a start.

"Yeah," said the boy. "Looks good, doesn't it?" He stroked the black camera frame with his thumb. "I bought this with my own lawn-mowing money."

Sammie eyed him with new interest. That's how she'd bought her binoculars—with her dog-walking money. But she wasn't about to tell him that.

"My dad bought me the extra lens, though," added the boy. "I took it off for that shot. Here's one with the lens on."

The camera gave a few muffled beeps as he pressed buttons. "Lookit."

A handsome black-and-white bird with a black cap was on the screen. *He was taking pictures of birds?*

"A black-and-white warbler!" she exclaimed.

"Nuh-uh," said the boy. "That's a blackpoll warbler."

"It is not," retorted Sammie before she could think better of it.

"It is too. Look, it's got a solid black cap over its whole head."

Sammie felt her cheeks flush as she examined the photo. It probably *was* a blackpoll warbler. She'd never seen one. Why did this boy have to be such a know-it-all? She felt a surge of dislike.

At that moment, she lost her grip on her notebook and it dropped to her feet, falling open.

The boy reached it first and picked it up. "Hey," he said, examining it. "That's a pretty good drawing."

"Give that back!"

"No, wait," said the boy. He turned a few pages in a leisurely way. "Wow, you take a lot of notes. Look at all this."

Sammie wanted to snatch it from him. No one, no one *ever* was allowed to look at her notebook. But if she grabbed it, she might tear the pages. She decided to try to be nice. "Can you give that back, please?"

"You know . . ." The boy pulled a pencil out of his back

pocket. "Your birds would come out better if you just—"
Lightly and rapidly he began to sketch alongside one of her
drawings. "See, the way their legs connect, you've got to get
the knee up close to the body—"

"Give it *back!*" Sammie shouted. "I don't care! I like my
birds the way they are."

"I was just trying to help," said the boy. He held out her
notebook.

"You're a know-it-all," said Sammie, snatching it back and
hugging it to her chest. She felt ready to cry. He had drawn
in her treasured notebook, he had invaded her Field, and she
hated boys anyway. "I'm going home." She ran up the path,
but halfway to her bike she paused. "This is *my* place!" she
yelled over her shoulder. "Don't forget it!"

WEATHER: Warm (enough for shorts and T-shirt!)
LOCATION: The Field
TIME: 4:00 p.m.

Entry woods, a warbler
(I think). Song:

rising trill broken
off at top.
Too high in trees
to spot!

Found under wooden door

edges are black

reddish-
brown
patches

just-molted skin collected

Growing around the door:

also lupine

sweet fern—
a hip-height
bush

leaf smells
sweet when
you crush it

purple/lavender
flowers

supposedly good for
bug bites, poison ivy &
burns—and also tea!

from a distance
lots of flower
spikes

3

FiFTH GRADE AND FROG FIGHTS

Sammie sat at her desk under the classroom's big window. Beyond, the spring day glittered like a fish's scales, beckoning her. The window seemed close enough to leap out. If only she could. She would run past the fringe of trees at the back of the playground, straight through the web of neighborhood streets until she reached the Field. It couldn't be more than a mile from here.

She sighed and turned back to the classroom. The voice of her teacher droned on, and a carpeted wasteland stretched from Sammie to the blackboard. Nothing enlivened this view. Not a fish tank, not even a potted plant. Just the scraps of student projects on the walls, and one of her poems, hanging right in the middle.

Emily, who sat at the desk in front of hers, was printing the answers onto the class worksheet. Emily's notebooks were always covered with doodles of hearts and flowers. As

Sammie watched, Emily stopped working and began drawing another flower. Sammie grimaced. As if flowers really looked like that: a circle for the middle and five big cartoon loops for petals.

Flowers, Sammie knew, were made of delicate silk that waved upward from a tucked-in dark center. In that center lay the heart of the flower: pollen-filled stamen stationed like flags around a tall, sticky pistil. Deeper still lay pockets of watery nectar, where bees thrust their long mouthparts as they kicked their feet against the pollen. Kids like Emily only knew how to squeal in terror when a bee flew into the classroom, shrieking, "Kill it! Kill it!" Sammie always hurried to catch every bee and bug that made its way inside before it met that fate and quickly released it back out the window.

On Sammie's first day at this new school, during recess, Emily had dutifully walked up to where Sammie was eagerly exploring the grassy verge at the playground's edge. Perhaps she'd been told by the teacher to be nice to the new girl.

"Would you like to hang out with us?" she said. "Adrien's teaching us how to make fishtail braids."

Sammie had studied her. That sounded pretty dull, and she was busy. "No, thank you," she said as politely as possible.

"Are you sure?" said Emily, frowning.

"Yes," said Sammie. "Perfectly sure. I like being by myself."

Emily had looked at her like she'd grown an extra head.

"What are you going to do all by yourself?"

Sammie wasn't sure she wanted to explain. The kids at her old school weren't interested in nature, and Sammie didn't like the way they blundered around, scaring off everything she wanted to see. She'd learned it was best to watch nature alone. But she took the plunge anyway.

"I'm looking for insects," she said, "so I can identify what's here."

"Oh." Emily's lips wrinkled in an expression of distaste. "Bugs. Gross." She stalked away.

They're not gross! Sammie had wanted to shout, but Emily was already rejoining her friends.

Now, carefully, Sammie withdrew her notebook from her desk and put it onto her lap. Normally she left it at home so no one else would look at it. But after yesterday's run-in at the Field, she wanted it close to her.

Making sure no one was watching, she opened to the page with the boy's drawing.

The bird perched in a sprightly way. Its head was cocked. Its feet curled into balls around a twig suggested by a single streak. He had sketched it hastily in just a few lines.

It was a good drawing, she had to admit it.

But this was *her* notebook. How dare he draw in it?

Sammie was still frowning at the page when she realized

someone was watching her. She looked up with a start. From a few desks away, Robert, her least favorite person in the world, was staring at her and grinning. He must have finished his worksheet—or, just as likely, left it blank.

Sammie jerked her eyes away before he could do anything mean. She was glad her notebook was hidden below her desk. She closed it and tucked it away.

If only the kids here would just ignore her like the kids at her old school. But soon after Emily and the popular girls had decided Sammie was weird for watching bugs alone on the playground, Robert had gotten in on the action.

Everyone knew about Robert. He was always the kid getting in trouble with the teachers. He got bad grades as if on purpose, and he was mean. Sammie knew he'd once put gum in Amy's beautiful, silky blond hair, so her mom was forced to cut it off.

It hadn't taken him long to single out Sammie as easy pickings. You'd think the other kids would take Sammie's side against the class bully, but instead they seemed relieved he'd found a new target.

By lunchtime, big clouds rolled over the sky and opened into a cloudburst. Just Sammie's luck—recess would be indoors today, and she probably wouldn't make it to the Field, either.

During recess, her head was buried in a book when

Robert waved a closed hand near her face. "I've got your frogs," he taunted.

He held a fistful of little clay forms.

For a class project, Sammie had made a diorama about spring peepers: frogs that come out each spring and make a huge racket down in the marsh.

She'd been so proud of her diorama, which had index cards carefully printed with information on the life cycle of spring peepers and was adorned with small painted clay frogs. It stood on a table on one side of the room with all the other kids' class projects. As usual, Mrs. Gladwell had put Sammie's project right in the center in a place of honor. When she'd first started school here in the fall, she'd always been pleased to have her work displayed so prominently, but now she cringed whenever Mrs. Gladwell exclaimed how impressive it was right in front of the rest of the class.

It always made Robert pick on her with extra ferocity— like right now.

"Put those back," Sammie said. She jumped up from her seat and lunged for her frogs. Robert swung out of the way, but she grabbed his other wrist. He waved his handful of frogs over her head. She jumped, trying to reach them.

"Mark," called Robert. "Catch!" He tossed the handful of frogs to Mark.

Mark caught one, and the rest scattered all over the rug.

"My frogs!" cried Sammie. She let go of Robert and dropped to her hands and knees to collect them. All three scrambled for frogs. She got a few, and Mark got a couple more.

"Give them *back!*" shouted Sammie.

This project was special, because her mom had for once found some time to help her with it. Sammie had painted the inside of a shoebox with infinite care: the bottom was blue for pond water, the back and sides green for the weedy shore. She cut paper into strips of reeds and pasted stones on the bottom of the box to represent a stony bank. And then the frogs, her pièce de résistance—which her mom said was French for "best part of all." Her mother had showed her how to make old-fashioned modeling clay: two cups of flour, one cup of water, a teaspoon of baking soda, and one cup of salt. Sammie had formed little rounded ovals, and when they were dry, she'd painted eyes and a slim brown X—the mark of spring peepers—on each one.

In real life, spring peepers were no bigger than a nickel but so loud that when close by they made your ears ring. Their high, bell-like calls were one of her favorite things about spring.

Now Mark grinned and waved her clay frogs.

Sammie flung herself on him. Her force knocked him over, and, sitting on him, she scrabbled for her frogs. From the corner of her eye, she could see Robert headed toward her diorama again. It made her desperate. She clawed at Mark's hand. "Ouch!" he said. "Get off me!" She pried his fingers open and pulled her frogs out.

"Sammie!" Her teacher's outraged voice cut through the fray. "Stop that right now!"

Everyone froze. Sammie felt all the eyes in the classroom on her. She stood up, breathing hard and flushed red.

Mrs. Gladwell was already crossing the room.

"I expect better of you! *Never* do that again—tackling your classmates is off-limits!"

"But—" A sense of injustice welled in Sammie's throat. "But Mark and Robert took my frogs!"

She looked around, wild-eyed and embarrassed. Robert had prudently broken off his pilgrimage for more frogs. Mark was sitting up, empty-handed. Two frogs lay on the floor.

"We were just looking at them, Mrs. Gladwell," said Robert.

Mrs. Gladwell eyed him. "Leave Sammie's science project alone," she snapped. "If I catch you touching it again, you'll get a detention."

"As for you." She frowned at Sammie. "That's ten minutes off next recess for you. We can't have brawling in the classroom. Never again, you hear me?"

Sammie stared at the floor.

"Whatever Mark and Robert did, that's no excuse for attacking them," Mrs. Gladwell went on. "Next time, come tell me instead. Now go sit down."

"Little Miss Perfect got in trouble," whispered Robert as she passed on her way to her seat.

Sammie's cheeks burned, and her eyes felt hot and stinging. She sat down and tried to hide her brimming tears by searching for a book inside her desk. She didn't want anyone to look at her, to witness her humiliation.

She glanced over to make sure Robert wasn't looking anymore. Then she slid her notebook back out of her desk. She opened to the page with the intruding sketch, grabbed a pencil, and angrily erased the boy's drawing.

For just one moment, she felt satisfaction. Then shame rose in her. It had been such a well-drawn bird. And now it was gone.

She pushed the notebook back into her desk. What a rotten day.

BRAM

By the next afternoon, the rain had cleared. Sammie slowed her bike as she approached the entrance to the Field, scanning the underbrush for any signs of disturbance: shifted branches, footprints in the wet dirt, someone else's bike. Nothing she could make out. That boy wouldn't be here today, she reassured herself. And if he turned up, she could leave.

She pushed through the brush and walked down the trail through the woods. The opening in the trees yawned ahead of her, sunny and free. She could see the Field sloping beyond. What a relief. No one.

She stepped out from the trees onto the sandy path.

Then she saw him. Sitting to the side, on a large boulder. A clump of trees had hidden him.

Sammie wheeled around to go back up the path.

"Wait," said the boy.

Sammie paused mid-step but still with her back to him, prepared to keep going.

"I'm sorry I wrote in your notebook," he called.

Sammie turned back and studied him. There he sat on the boulder, wearing floppy khaki shorts and an old T-shirt, his camera in his lap. Sammie herself had sat there many times, gazing down at the gold-green Field beyond.

"Really?" she said.

"Yeah," he said. "It wasn't very thoughtful of me."

How else could Sammie respond? "It's okay," she said.

"I really liked your notebook," said the boy. "If I promise not to write in it, can I look at it again?"

Sammie gave him a long stare. She thought about the blackpoll warbler on his camera screen the day before. She thought about Robert.

"No," she said finally.

"Maybe you could hold it and show me a few pages."

"Why do you care?" said Sammie.

"I just thought it was cool."

That was different. No one had ever said that to her before.

"Swear you won't try to take it," she said.

"I swear," said the boy.

"Swear you won't touch it at all."

"I swear," he said. "I'll shake on it." He held out his hand. Sammie stepped closer, reached out, and shook it. His skin felt cool against her palm, which was hot from biking. Then, slowly, she reached back to unzip her pack, tugged out her notebook, and opened it so he could see.

The boy read carefully, moving his hand occasionally to ask her to turn the pages. Her heart was bumping against her chest like a caged sparrow. Her notebook's open pages felt like they bared her soul.

"It's so great how you write down everything you see," he said. "And the weather and everything. I never thought about doing that."

The praise smote Sammie with pleasure and surprise. Then, without thinking about it, she turned the page one more time—to the one with a smudge where his bird had been. Oh no! She had forgotten, and now he was sure to be upset.

"I'm sorry I erased your bird!" she burst out.

The boy raised both dark brown eyebrows. His face held nothing but mild surprise.

"My bird?" he said, sounding puzzled. "Oh, that!" He waved an airy hand. "That bird wasn't any good—it was just an example. I don't draw anymore. Drawing takes too long, and it isn't *real*."

He fingered his camera, smiling at it in satisfaction.

Sammie would never forgive someone who erased her drawings. She thought drawings were as good as any photograph. She was about to say so when he looked up suddenly.

"What's your name, anyway? I'm Bram."

"Sammie."

"Sammie," repeated Bram, his face serious, like he was making sure to remember. "Do you really come here every day?"

"Yeah." She looked at him guardedly.

"That's cool! You probably know a whole lot about this place."

"I know everything about it," said Sammie. She squinted at him. "Wait. You said you come here every day, too."

"Oh, only for the past week or so in the mornings. The light's better for photography then. But now I'm back at school, so I started coming in the afternoons." At Sammie's uncomprehending frown, he added, "I just moved here. From Seattle."

"Oh! You're new."

"Yep," said Bram. "My parents gave me a few days to get used to it here, but then they made me start school."

"But I haven't seen you there, either," said Sammie. "Aren't you in fifth grade?"

"Sixth," said Bram.

One of the big kids, thought Sammie. At Sammie's school, sixth graders got special privileges, like first-period recess and their own lockers.

"I wish I didn't have to go," said Bram. He looked out over the Field with a slightly furrowed brow, his glasses reflecting a glint of spring light. "I can learn more outdoors."

"Same here!" Sammie exclaimed.

Bram grinned. "Hey, you should show me around this place. We could bird-watch together."

He was the first kid, ever, who'd wanted to join her in nature watching. Yet a surge of reluctance rose in Sammie. She didn't like the idea of letting someone else in on her hard-won secret world. She thought of the spot at the edge of the woods where sometimes she curled up to watch for hours with her back against a tree trunk. She thought about the old door and how once she'd even found a mouse under there. It had stared up with glistening black eyes, motionless, before abruptly scooting away into the underbrush.

"How come you moved from Seattle?"

"My dad's job ended," said Bram. He sighed, the first time she'd seen his face look anything but cheerful. "He's a physicist. He's an assistant professor at the university here now."

"My dad works at the university, too!" exclaimed Sammie. "In computer support."

As soon as she said it, she wished she hadn't. Bram's dad was a professor. A scientist, for real. Maybe Bram wouldn't think much of someone who just fixed the computers. Her dad had tried to start his own consulting company, but it hadn't worked out. He'd been unemployed for more than a year—this job, he'd said, was the best he could find. It's why they'd moved here.

But Bram's face brightened.

"Hey, that's cool! We should introduce them to each other."

Sammie relaxed a bit. "Yeah, maybe."

"We had a great cabin near Seattle," he said, looking dreamily into space. "Out there they've got the biggest trees you'll ever see. Cedars so big you need climbing gear to get up them. Three grown-ups can barely reach all the way around the trunk. And through all those trees you could see the ocean. Man, there's nothing better than the ocean! I could take photographs of it all day long. It smells salty and sweet. You breathe in and the air is perfectly clear. Just a little salt to wake you up and get your mind going."

His eyes had a faraway look. "We had to sell our cabin when my dad switched jobs."

His words had drawn Sammie in. He talked as enthusiastically as she used to before she realized other kids found it strange. She took a deep breath. "That's too bad."

"I miss Seattle," he said. "There's no water here. Just hills and fields on and on."

"There is *too* water here!" said Sammie. "There's a great pond."

"A pond's nothing compared to the ocean," said Bram.

"How do *you* know what the Pond is like? It has things no ocean has," said Sammie. She didn't know much about the ocean; she only visited once a summer. But she wasn't about to let Bram criticize it. "I'll prove it to you. Come on."

She marched down the path. Bram hopped off the boulder and followed.

Halfway down, Sammie turned into the low brush. This weed-choked route would take them to one of the more hidden, magical spaces of the Field.

She seldom had time to go to the Pond, because she needed to get home before her mother did to avoid awkward questions. But now, too eager to worry about the time, she pushed determinedly through the weeds.

"Wait, stop!" exclaimed Bram.

He was still standing on the path.

"I can't go in there."

"Why not?" demanded Sammie.

"Poison ivy," said Bram. "Tons of it! Aren't you scared to walk through there?"

Sammie looked around in surprise. "I walk here all the time," she said.

"Wow," he said, shaking his head. "You must not be allergic."

Sammie waded back out. Bram pointed to a lanky plant that came up to Sammie's knees and bore many triplets of shiny green leaves. "Leaves of three, let it be," he said.

One more thing Bram knew that Sammie didn't. She'd learned about a lot of wildflowers but had never paid attention to this lowly green vine.

"Then how am I supposed to show you the Pond?" she said.

"Hm. Follow me." Bram strolled farther down the path.

Sammie trailed him. It annoyed her how he wanted to take charge.

"Let's go through here and then backtrack. There's just grass, no poison ivy."

"We can't go down there. It leads to the Junkyard House. It scares me."

She pointed out the roof to Bram, just visible past the saplings at the bottom of the slope.

Bram squinted down at it through his zoom lens. "Well," he said, "maybe I can go in through the poison ivy part if I wear long pants and make sure I wash them after."

"All right," said Sammie. "Let's meet back here tomorrow."

"Okay." They trooped back to the top of the Field. At the path's end, they said goodbye and parted ways, Bram taking the road off to the left on foot, and Sammie pointing her bicycle to the right to head back home.

Only halfway there did she realize that she had actually *invited* him back to her Field. In her fervor to prove it was as good as Seattle, she'd forgotten all about not showing it to him.

Well, she thought, *it's only once.*

WEATHER: Cool, breezy
LOCATION: The Field, entry woods
TIME: 3:30 p.m.

At the entrance to the Field:

Two doves on a phone wire
Teeter in the wind
They welcome me like sentinels
The afternoon begins

Mourning doves on a telephone wire

Female downy head pattern

Every downy woodpecker has a different pattern on the back of its head

DOWNY WOODPECKER

The entry woods some days seem to have just as many birds as the whole rest of the Field. So much birdsong today!

male would have a red patch

tap-tap-tapping on a dead bough

WHITE-BREASTED NUTHATCH
on a tree branch singing "ank-ank."
Nuthatches always creep <u>down</u>
the trunk or branch

5

CAMP

Sammie was sitting on a stool in the kitchen while her mom braided her hair. Sammie could braid it herself, but she liked the feeling of her mother's sure fingers pulling the strands into place. It was one of the only times, ever since they'd moved here and her mom had started working at the post office, when Sammie could feel her mom's whole attention on her.

Thin decorative mirrors along the window reflected them both. Sammie studied her mom's small frown, the way the edges of her mouth turned down. Probably not the best time to bother her.

"Do I have to go to school today?" said Sammie anyway. The hairbrush softly scritch-scratched her head.

"What kind of a question is that?" asked her mother. "Of course you do."

A chickadee flitted to the bird feeder suction-cupped to

the window, plucked a sunflower seed from the mix, and nipped away. At this time of year, maybe it would carry the seed to a brood of tiny fuzzy chickadee babies.

Sammie wasn't sure how she'd turned out so different from her own parents. Her mom was small and plump with brown hair in a short practical bob. Her dad had black hair and was tall and, unlike her mom, tanned easily. He didn't get out in the sun much, though—he preferred to spend his time lost in thought at his computer. Sammie was medium tall for her age, and her hair was yellow as the sun.

And she'd managed to pick up from each parent what was least like the other. Like her dad, she enjoyed classifying and figuring things out—but he preferred to build stuff, whether a computer program or a shelf in the hall. Meanwhile, Sammie had learned her interest in nature from her mom's bird feeder and houseplants and carefully tended garden. But her mom didn't have Sammie's craving to *understand* everything, to dig right down until she knew nature as intimately as a wild animal does.

"I learn more when I stay home." After Sammie spoke, she realized she'd repeated almost exactly what that boy Bram had said the day before.

"School's almost over for the summer," said her mom crisply. "Oh, and I have great news! You'll like this." Her mom's expression brightened, and she sounded excited.

"Yeah?" Sammie felt hope rise inside her.

"I found a summer camp for you."

"Camp?" Sammie blinked. "What camp?"

"Camp Shriver, it's called, a day camp. I've heard a lot of the kids from your school go there. They do arts and crafts and swimming and sports. You'll get home right when I'm back from work, so you won't be alone as much. It'll be so much better."

Sammie's heart went cold.

She knew about Camp Shriver. The kids at school were already talking about it. Would she have to spend her whole glorious summer with the same kids who made her life so miserable? If she and her mom arrived home at the same time, she wouldn't even have afternoons at the Field.

"You're going to love it," her mom was saying happily. "And maybe it would be a chance to make some friends, Sammie."

"I don't want to go to camp," said Sammie flatly. "I don't want to be around the other kids from school."

"Oh, Sammie, come now," said her mom. Her frown reappeared, and the lines around her mouth. "It won't be anything like school, you'll see. Things will be different in a relaxed environment."

"All the other kids think I'm weird."

Her mom sighed. "You're so much like your dad,

Sammie—you live in your own head. Why don't you try being a little friendlier to them?"

Sammie's thoughts flew back to her diorama and her "brawl," as Mrs. Gladwell had called it, with Robert and Mark. Her throat squeezed. She couldn't tell her mom about that—she might get in trouble for fighting.

"I want to stay here this summer," she said instead. "I have things to do."

"Sweetheart, I just can't leave you on your own all day. It's bad enough that I have to let you come home alone every afternoon right now. I worry about you. What would you do all day by yourself?"

Sammie hesitated.

"I don't know. Bird-watch. Read. Like I do after school. Besides"—she had a brainstorm—"I have a new friend now. His name is Bram. He lives in the neighborhood."

So that was a bit of a lie. Bram wasn't exactly her *friend*.

"You do? Oh, I'm glad to hear that, honey. You should invite him over."

Sammie gave a noncommittal grunt.

Her mom wasn't distracted long. "Still, you're going to need something to do this summer. I thought you'd love the idea of camp."

"Well, I don't! I wish you could just stay home like you used to."

"Oh, Sammie, I *know* you do." Her mom sounded hurt, and Sammie felt badly immediately. "We've talked about this before."

Her mom wrapped the elastic around Sammie's braid and then walked around to face her, putting her hands on Sammie's shoulders and looking earnestly into her eyes. Sammie had already heard this so many times since they'd moved to this rickety house, and here it came again.

"I really, really wish I could, Sammie. I know it's been hard. For me, too. But this is where your dad could find work, and we owe so much on this house. I have to help."

Sammie swallowed. "I know."

"And, Sammie, learning how to deal with other people is part of growing up." Her mom firmly patted her shoulder, then gave it an encouraging little shake. "You'll find ways to connect with the other kids if you keep trying, sweetheart." Then she stood up straight, her stance showing that the matter was closed. Sammie could see her mom was trying to convey one of her "life lessons" that never felt like they actually fit Sammie's life.

Sammie didn't think she needed other people at all. She needed animals and plants and the outdoors. Someday she would be a scientist and spend all her time studying nature and making discoveries on her own.

"Please give camp a chance, Sammie." Her mom was

looking at her with an expression Sammie knew all too well, full of expectation.

Sammie gave a fractional nod. What else could she do?

"That's my mighty girl," said her mother, kissing her forehead. "Come on now." She went right back to being her usual practical, bustling self, popping Sammie's thermos into her lunch box and zipping it up. "You'll miss the bus."

Standing at the corner, waiting for the bus to school, Sammie sighed. Didn't her mom realize she was mighty enough to stay home on her own? She'd just turned eleven— she wasn't a little kid anymore. She didn't need Camp Shriver and to have her days planned out.

If she were gone all summer, what if Bram spent all *his* days at the Field? What if by the time she got back, it had become *his* place?

No one understood her, she thought bitterly. Then the bus pulled up, and she tightened her backpack straps and got on.

6
THE MUSKRAT POND

How did Bram always get to the Field first?

Standing stiffly by the boulder, he wore jeans, hiking boots, and woolen socks pulled over his pants all the way to his knees. His long-sleeved shirt was tightly tucked in at the waist. He was even wearing a pair of cotton gardening gloves.

"You look ready," said Sammie dryly.

Bram didn't catch her sarcasm. "I am ready," he said, looking very serious.

"Aren't you baking hot?"

"No," said Bram. "I'm used to it. It's not that warm today anyway."

It was one of those spring days when wind blows big clouds across the sky—warm with the sun out, cool when it went behind the clouds. Sunlight skittered over the Field, now bright, now dark again. The pine trees blazed like green candles when the sun struck them.

"Besides," said Bram, "this will keep ticks off, too."

"Ticks? Oh, I never worry about them."

"You should," said Bram in an older-brother kind of voice. "They carry Lyme disease. My mom always checks my hair for ticks when I get home."

I can't ask my mom to do that, thought Sammie. "Well, if there are any, my mom would spot them when she braids my hair."

Bram eyed her. "You should wear long socks and pants."

Sammie didn't like Bram telling her what to do.

As usual Bram had his camera around his neck. Now he slung it across his shoulder and hugged it against his body with his elbow. "Anyway, I can check you for them later. Let's go," he said.

Sammie always followed a narrow path—maybe a deer trail—through the weeds. It was choked by new spring growth. After a hesitation, Bram plunged in after her.

Slogging through thigh-high brush, they reached one of Sammie's favorite stopping points. Here, two solidly built apple trees, left over from when this whole area might've been farm fields or a rural garden, stood half-smothered by shrubs and wild vines. Their blossoms crowned the thicket— two different varieties, a white waterfall to the left, a pink powder puff on the right.

Sammie smiled up at the white one. Sunlight filtered

through the flowers, and a hum of bees warmed the afternoon. "My favorite apple tree," she said. "It was packed with apples in the fall. When they're ripe, they're sort of streaky yellow and brown. They're lumpy, but they're tart and sweet."

"I'm more interested in this one," said Bram, fingering the blooms of the pink tree. "Crab apples. When they're ripe, the birds will come for them."

"The regular apples will be just as good for critters when they fall," insisted Sammie. "Skunks and deer, I bet." She daydreamed. "Maybe even a bear."

"There won't be bears here," scoffed Bram. "Too many houses, and not enough places like this with trees and shrubs and wetlands. Back at our cabin, we used to get black bears all the time."

"Well, you never know," said Sammie, but she knew he was right. She'd never heard of a bear in this town. They'd been driven out by development long ago.

At that moment, a scrap of orange floated past the swarm of blossoms. "A monarch!" she exclaimed. "The first one of the year! Last summer there were lots of them."

The butterfly drifted like a leaf on the May breeze. It was the size of Sammie's outstretched palm as she reached up toward it.

"Do you have these in Seattle?" asked Sammie, hoping they didn't.

"Sure we do," said Bram. "We learned in school that monarchs migrate all the way to Mexico."

Sammie shook her head in wonder. "It's kind of hard to believe something so tiny could make such a big journey, isn't it?"

"My dad always says the smallest things are the strongest," said Bram. "Like bonds between atoms. Nothing's connected more tightly."

"I guess so," said Sammie. When Robert and Mark were bullying her at school, she felt small and not very strong at all. She felt a lot like that butterfly looked: helpless and wind-blown and carried along by things beyond her control.

As if to guide them, the monarch fluttered off in the direction of the Pond. They glanced at each other and continued behind it.

After twenty minutes, the weeds gave way to a thicket of thin, whippy trees.

"What the heck are these?" said Bram, shoving between them. "Do they have to grow so close together?"

"They're alders," said Sammie, proud to finally teach Bram something. "See their catkins? They like damp places like this."

Bram was breathing hard. "Man, this place isn't easy to get to, is it?"

Sammie was too busy struggling with a net of interlaced branches to answer.

At last, they saw it: glimmering water, ringed by pond plants. The Pond sat right in the lowest part of the valley. On the farther side, opposite the Field, the ground sloped up into a pine and oak forest.

The bank was fringed by slender maples and birches. Not far from where they stood, one large tree had tipped, leaning over the water.

"Hey, look," said Sammie. "A muskrat lodge."

A rounded heap of sticks and twigs humped up from the water, like someone had dropped a very large and messy hat.

"Maybe we'll see the muskrat," said Bram.

"We made a lot of noise coming down," said Sammie. "Next time we should be quieter."

"Quieter?" Bram snorted. He looked back toward the alder grove, his expression reading to Sammie like disapproval. "Getting here was like bushwhacking a jungle."

"I always at least try," said Sammie. Why was Bram so judgmental?

"What we *should* do is sit awhile. The muskrat will forget we're here," said Bram. "That's how I get my best photos."

"I don't have time to wait," said Sammie frostily. "I have to go home soon. *I* always walk quietly."

She was irritated as much with herself as with Bram. She should have talked less, reminded him to set his feet down gently. She'd been distracted by having a new person with her. It was better, after all, to come here alone.

But maybe there was still a way she could show off the Pond.

"I've got a collecting box in my pack. Let's get some water!" Her box was empty—she always made sure to remove her specimens after each expedition. "It's clear, so we'll be able to see through the plastic. I read that at this time of year there'll be lots of pond bugs."

"Invertebrates," corrected Bram.

"Invertebrates. Yeah, duh. That's what I meant." Sammie frowned. Stupid know-it-all Bram.

Where they stood, a group of waist-high young cattails blocked access to the Pond. Sammie eyed the leaning tree, its upper branches dipping into the water.

"Watch," she said. She jumped onto the base of the tilted trunk.

Wriggling past a knot of branches, she stood and began walking. The narrow trunk was barely wider than her shoes, but Sammie was an expert tree climber. She kept her balance by holding on to smaller twigs as she hurried along.

Where the trunk drooped toward the water, she knelt and opened the collecting box. Then she reached down, her hand clamped around the rectangular plastic container.

"Careful, you're going to fall," said Bram.

"No, I'm not." She could get only the very edge of the box into the water.

"Don't you think that's good enough?"

"No, hang on," insisted Sammie. "I want to get down into the weeds where things live."

Beside her a branch jutted outward. She grabbed hold of it and dangled to lean almost completely upside down, plunging the box elbow-deep into water thick with reeds.

"There!"

And then, for the first time in her life, Sammie fell out of a tree.

7

PAINTERS AND PHOTOGRAPHERS

Tumbling off the trunk, she landed with a colossal splash, squelching straight into the sticky, seemingly bottomless muck of the pond. The branch had snapped. Instead of a good strong living limb, she realized too late, it was a rickety dried-up specimen of former life.

She came gasping and furious back up from the water's surface. She stood knee-deep in muck and water, hands covered in mud, hair plastered to her grimy forehead, weeds dangling off her arms, still clutching the collecting box. Bram stared in astonishment. Then he began howling with laughter.

"Shut up!" spluttered Sammie. "You big dork! Shut up!"

"I'm sorry," wheezed Bram. "It's just— It's just—"

Sammie glowered, wiping water from under her nose.

Bram recovered his composure and reached out a hand. "You want some help out?"

Sammie slogged her way to the bank. She pushed past Bram's outstretched hand and hauled herself to dry land.

"You're drenched," said Bram more sympathetically. "We'd better get you home."

"I can't go home!" said Sammie. "My parents will kill me."

"They will? Why?"

"I'm not supposed to be in the Field," said Sammie. "My mom says I'm not allowed."

Bram's black brows drew together. "Oh."

"I'll have to wait until I get dry," said Sammie miserably. She was chilled—the breeze was biting through her clothes—and worried. After walking all the way to the Pond, she might not get home before her mom. How long would it take her to dry, and how could she avoid her mom noticing all this mud?

"You can come to my house," said Bram. "My mom can get you fixed up."

"Really?"

"Yeah, of course!"

"She won't make me tell my mom?"

"Why would she? She won't even think of it. Come on."

The two of them hurried back up the brushy path. After collecting Sammie's bike, they continued a block and a half before Bram turned into a driveway. "Here it is," he said.

"You live really close!" said Sammie, her teeth chattering.

No wonder Bram made it to the Field so early every day.

"That's the other good thing about coming to my place."

Bram's house was smaller than Sammie's. It was a split-level, painted blue, partly stuck into the hill behind it. Bram opened the door. From the landing, stairs led up and down.

"Ma?" called Bram.

"In the kitchen!" came a voice.

Bram led Sammie up a short staircase to the main floor, right at ground level in the back. The lower floor had to be mostly belowground.

In the kitchen, a tall woman was standing at the stove. Bram's mother had long silky black hair that hung to the middle of her back, and she wore a sleeveless shirt and paint-stained blue jeans. On her forearm, she had a tattoo of a spray of pink blossoms on a black branch. Sammie had never met anyone with a tattoo before.

"Ma, this is my friend Sammie," said Bram. "She fell in the pond. Can you help get her dry?"

Bram's mother turned down the burner and looked up. Immediately her face shifted into concern as she took in Sammie's bedraggled state.

"Oh, you poor thing!" she said. "Bram, how could you let your friend fall in the pond?" Sammie felt annoyed—Bram hadn't *let* her fall in the pond. She'd done it all by her own show-off self. But his mom's tone was light and teasing, and without expecting an answer, she stepped forward and put one slim arm around Sammie's shoulders. "Come with me, honey. Bram, you stay here."

In the hall, Bram's mother pulled a thick towel out of the linen closet and wrapped Sammie in it, rubbing her energetically. She patted the bathroom door. "Go ahead and get cleaned up. You'll have to wear Bram's clothes while I pop yours in the dryer."

When Sammie had taken off her wet things, Bram's mother pushed the bathroom door partway open and handed in an armful of clothes—soft sweatpants and a shirt. They were much too big but warm and comfortable.

Bram was sitting on a stool in the kitchen, turning slowly in a circle and pushing buttons on the camera in his lap. When Sammie came in, his mouth curled up at the corner.

"*Don't* say anything," warned Sammie.

Bram just grinned. "You want some cookies?" He hopped down, opened a cabinet, and began rummaging.

"Don't we have to ask your mom?" said Sammie.

"Nah," said Bram. "My mom says it's my responsibility to know when to stop eating sweets. 'If you feel sick, it's not my fault,' she says."

Sammie took this in, boggled.

"She's probably already forgotten we're here and gone back to work. She's a painter. She's always thinking about art."

Unlike the big comfortable wooden table at Sammie's, this kitchen had a raised counter with stools around it. She climbed onto one, holding up the baggy sweatpants and taking the chance to look around. This house was small but updated and stylish, with modern art on the walls that looked to Sammie more like blocks and scribbles of color than what she usually thought of as "art." It didn't look a bit like the cozy clutter of teapots, quilted hangings, house-plants, and assorted bric-a-brac Sammie's mom decorated the kitchen with. Instead, it looked like something out of a fancy magazine.

Bram brought a box of chocolate-covered cookies to the kitchen counter. As he filled two tall glasses with milk, Sammie watched in greedy surprise. Her mother would never have let her eat cookies before dinner.

The sliding-glass door let out into an enclosed patio crowded with canvases, cans of paintbrushes, and an easel. Paint splotches dotted the floor. Bram's mother wasn't in there. Sammie wondered where she was working.

"Your mom's so cool," said Sammie a little enviously.

Bram nibbled a cookie. "I guess," he said, and sighed. "She's pretty spaced-out a lot of the time. She works every second of the day."

"At least she's at home," countered Sammie. "My mom even works weekends."

Just then Bram's mother loped up the stairs and into the room. "I rinsed the mud out of your clothes and put them through a spin cycle, Sammie. They're in the dryer now."

"Thanks so much, um . . ." Sammie paused.

"Vicky," said Bram's mom. "Bram, get Sammie's clothes for her once they're dry." She opened a pot on the stove and looked in. "Dinner will be ready in half an hour. You're welcome to stay, Sammie."

"Sammie's mom is expecting her," said Bram. Sammie nudged him, but it was too late.

"She can call home, if she likes," said Vicky. "Would you like to use the phone, dear?"

"No!" blurted Sammie. "I mean, no, um— I'll grab my stuff after fifteen minutes or so, if that's okay."

"Okay, honey. Whatever works for you."

Vicky's long strides took her out into the back porch. If Vicky had been more like her own mom, Sammie thought, she'd definitely have forced Sammie to call home.

"Wanna see my room?" said Bram.

Sammie drained her milk, grabbed one last cookie, and slid off the stool to follow Bram downstairs.

His bedroom was on the bottom floor. It had just one long thin window near the ceiling, looking out on the soil and plants of the front yard. Tufts of grass pressed against the pane.

Unlike the kitchen, the room looked like the result of a minor explosion. Clothes and objects lay scattered all over the floor, piled on the bed, heaped on the dresser and desk. Magnetic linking toys and LEGOs and K'NEX, built into various constructions. Colored paper, folded into geometric origami shapes. Pencils, books, paper, cables, USB drives, and other unidentifiable technological equipment. In one corner, a violin case rested against the wall. A music stand perched like a long-legged bird above the debris.

"It's chaos in here!" said Sammie.

Bram raised his brows. "Maybe it is a little messy," he admitted.

"You play violin?"

He made a face. "In an orchestra. But look."

He picked his way across the room to his desk and opened his laptop. With a humming wheeze it blinked to life.

Bram pulled out a cable and plugged in his camera. "Watch this."

For a moment, a warbler stood on his screen. Bram picked up a stylus, and with a few moves of the pen-like instrument against the screen, he bent the photo into a twisted whirlwind, less bird than hurricane. He grinned. "That's called a filter," he said. "Swirl, it's called. Cool, huh?"

Sammie stared at the distorted bird. "What good does that do?" she said.

"Well, that's just for fun. But I can do all kinds of other stuff. I can change the contrast, I can sharpen the focus. I can change how bright the sky is compared to the tree." He tapped and fiddled.

"I like things the way they really are," said Sammie.

"The camera can't make things exactly the way they are," said Bram. "This way I can make them the way I think they should be."

Sammie opened her mouth to disagree. *I thought you were complaining that drawing wasn't real,* she wanted to remind him. With a start, though, she noticed the time at the bottom of Bram's screen.

"Uh-oh. I have to go," she said.

The two of them hurried down the hall and fished out Sammie's half-dry clothing. Sammie ducked into the bathroom and changed.

At the front door, she paused.

"Are you coming tomorrow?" she said. As she spoke, she wasn't sure if she was asking Bram to come or just checking if he might.

"I can't," said Bram. "Saturdays my mom drives me into the city for violin. Want to meet up Sunday?" He looked hopeful. His friendly face couldn't help warming Sammie. He really had done her a favor today.

"My mom's home that morning, but she tutors in the

afternoon," she said. "And my dad never notices how long I'm gone—he's always too busy programming stuff on his computer. He gets so into it, he doesn't even hear if you say hi. My mom calls him our space cadet."

"I know what that's like. Okay. In the afternoon, then."

"We should bring a jar," said Sammie.

"Jar?"

"To get our pond water."

"You want to try that *again*?"

"I'm a scientist," said Sammie severely. "I don't give up just like that."

WEATHER: Cloudy, wet, warm
LOCATION: The Pond
TIME: 4:15 p.m.

Spotted catching insects
in the alders:

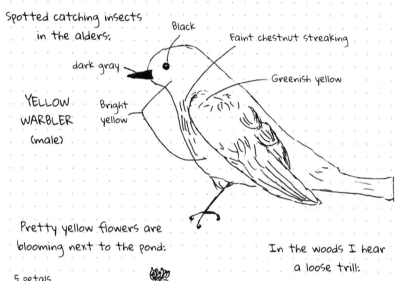

Black
Faint chestnut streaking
dark gray
Greenish yellow

YELLOW
WARBLER
(male)

Bright
yellow

Pretty yellow flowers are
blooming next to the pond:

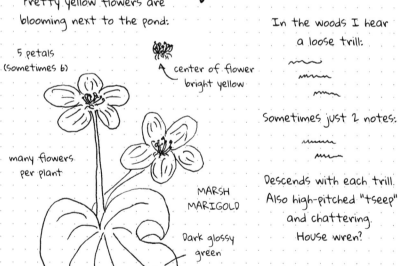

5 petals
(sometimes 6)

center of flower
bright yellow

many flowers
per plant

MARSH
MARIGOLD

Dark glossy
green

The leaves arise
from the base of each flower's stem

In the woods I hear
a loose trill:

Sometimes just 2 notes:

Descends with each trill.
Also high-pitched "tseep"
and chattering.
House wren?

Other species here: grackle,
house finch, titmouse,
Baltimore oriole, blue jay

8

BETTER PLANNING, BETTER LUCK

On Sunday morning, Sammie fished an empty glass pickle jar from the recycling. Then she hurried downstairs to the basement. Stuff no one really needed—or didn't need often—was stored down here, much of it still in boxes from the move.

In one corner stood a pile of mops, shovels, pruners, and other long-handled items. Just what she was looking for. After a struggle, she got one broom head unscrewed. She dropped its heap of straw hair next to the other tools. The handle was the prize.

Sammie tried to attach the jar to the long handle with string. But no matter how tightly wrapped, the string kept sliding off, even when she used glue. The jar was too heavy.

She tried wire. The wire slithered off just like the string.

Then she had an idea.

Avoiding her mother, who was sitting at the kitchen table

going through her tutoring materials, she crept upstairs and opened her mother's sock drawer. Lines of pantyhose neatly tucked in plastic compartments met her eyes. She stuffed one pair into her pocket. With cheeks pink with guilt, she shut the drawer and hurried back downstairs to the basement. She was used to hiding her activities from her mom by now, but stealing her clothes felt like a whole new level.

She slung one pantyhose foot over an end of the broom handle and pulled the leg all the way down to hook it at the other end. Then she pushed the jar down the other leg.

She wrapped wire around the pantyhose at the jar mouth. With scissors, she snipped a hole in one side of the pantyhose, pulling it just barely over the jar mouth. With a few more circles of wire, she held the pantyhose tightly in place. The jar dangled in the pantyhose leg off the handle's end, firmly held, with a hole for water to go in.

Perfect.

That afternoon, Sammie awkwardly mounted her bicycle and slung the pole over her shoulder, her bike wobbling and the jar swinging overhead.

At the Field, she found Bram dressed just like on Friday. "No poison ivy rash!" he crowed, looking pleased with himself. "Oh, good, you're in long pants, too. You should tuck them into your socks."

After all her hard work on the jar, that's what Bram noticed? His eyes widened, though, as she came closer.

"What on earth is *that*? It looks wacky!"

"It doesn't look any wackier than *you*," snapped Sammie. "It's a collecting pole."

She handed it over. Bram inspected it. "Will it work?"

"Of course," said Sammie with more confidence than she felt. "Let's go."

Their first visit to the Pond had flattened the grasses and pushed aside the brush, making this trip easier. The jar swung back and forth over Sammie's shoulder like a metronome.

At the Pond, the fallen tree shone in the spring light. It wasn't quite dead; young leaves glistened on its branches.

"Want me to do it?" said Bram.

"No." Sammie tightened her grip around the broom handle.

She climbed more cautiously this time. Then she clamped her knees around the trunk, tensing her muscles to anchor herself.

The collecting jar slid into the water with a satisfying *schlomp*. Sammie wouldn't fall this time—but she worried the jar would slip free of its wire loop.

Bram stood on the bank, shifting eagerly from foot to foot. "Run it along the bottom," he called. "That's where all the good stuff will be."

"I know," said Sammie shortly. "Don't be so impatient."

A sticky tug of muck and weeds sucked at the jar as she dragged its mouth along. But the wire stayed tight, tangled in the pantyhose. Hand over hand, she hauled the jar dripping from the water. Resting it on the tree trunk, she pulled the lid out of her pocket, tugged the wire off the jar mouth, and clapped the lid onto the jar, screwing it down.

"I got it!"

Bram stopped hopping back and forth long enough to snap a couple of photos of Sammie's triumph. "Great!"

Sammie edged back along the trunk and scrambled onto the bank. They knelt together to examine the jar. Sammie held it up to the light.

The debris was already settling: a mix of twigs, decaying leaves, clumps of algae, and muck drifting to the bottom of the jar. At the surface, a layer of clearer water was developing.

They watched. Tiny beings darted back and forth, almost indistinguishable from the muck around them except for their more definite paths of motion. "A water beetle!" exclaimed Bram. And there it swam, black and button-size, burrowing downward to clutch a twig, a bubble of air clinging to its abdomen to allow it to breathe.

"Look!" squealed Sammie. "A *hydra*!"

As the murk sank, it came into view: a tiny creature the length of a grain of rice but bright green as a lime lollipop. It looked like a twig, but on top it sported a headful of six ten-tacles, like a tiny medusa. The base of the hydra's stalk was attached to a broken stick. As Sammie and Bram stared, the creature bent, grabbed the stick with its tentacles, and did a somersault, planting the base of its stalk on the stick again.

"Aren't they *amazing*?" breathed Sammie, awed. After another couple of somersaults, the tiny animal halted at the end of the stick and reached its tendrils to search the water.

"I'd take a picture," exhaled Bram, "but the flash would reflect off the glass."

"If only we could go to my house. We could look at the water under the microscope," said Sammie.

"You have a microscope?"

"Yeah, I got it for Christmas."

"Wow!" said Bram. "How come we can't go to your place?"

"I don't want my parents asking questions about where we got the pond water."

"I thought your mom wasn't home."

"My dad's there."

"I bet he won't even notice the jar."

"But what if he does?"

"We can figure out something to say. Leave it to me."

Sammie didn't know if she trusted Bram. And she wasn't too sure she wanted him to see her house. The realtor had called it a "fixer-upper." It was tall and skinny and painted purple, with tall narrow windows like surprised eyes, and a funny, small attic room stuck on the very top. It was old and, despite her parents' best efforts, looked shabby.

She didn't want Bram making fun of it.

"Well . . ."

"Come on. It'd be so awesome to see this through the microscope."

It really would. If Bram decided to be mean, she'd know not to be his friend anymore.

"You have to swear not to say anything that will give us away."

"I swear," said Bram. "Really."

9

A MILLION TINY CREATURES

For months, Sammie had begged for a microscope. A real one, not like the low-magnification ones at school.

"It's too expensive, Sammie, sweetheart," said her mother wearily. "Maybe another year."

But then Sammie's dad had fixed the computer of a biology professor at the university who owned a microscope he didn't need anymore. Sammie's dad drove her out to his house to pick it up.

When her dad knocked on the door, a lean, craggy gentleman with white hair opened it. "Hi, Dave," said the professor. He eyed Sammie. "Come in," he said, seemingly to her in particular.

In the front hall, three lab coats hung from the coat rack. A line of muddy rubber boots occupied low shelves. The umbrella holder held fishing poles instead of umbrellas.

Framed X-ray prints of animal skeletons decorated the walls.

On a side table sat a microscope as big as Sammie's torso, with knobs and lenses poking out from all sides. Sammie stared at it hungrily but a little scared. Could she ever learn how to use that?

The old professor gripped it by the neck. He contemplated Sammie from under bushy eyebrows. "Have you ever used a microscope before?"

"Just the little ones at school," Sammie managed to say.

The old professor paused thoughtfully, then heaved the microscope from its place. "Come with me," he said.

They followed him down a dark hallway into a room of tidy bookshelves and glass cabinets full of shells, skeletons, and other curios. Wood cabinets held hundreds of labeled drawers. He opened one. It was crammed with specimens and prepared slides.

Sammie watched, rapt, as the old professor bent over the microscope, prepared a slide, and tucked it neatly between the calipers that held it to the microscope stage below the lens.

He switched on the microscope light and showed her the three different lenses that could be rotated into place for greater magnification: 10x, 40x, 100x. He showed her how to lower a cover slip—a small glass cover for the specimen—so no bubbles would form. He showed her how to focus first with the coarse magnification knob, then the fine one. "At high magnification, use just the fine-tuning knob," he instructed, "so you don't accidentally jam the lens against the slide and scratch it."

As she bent to the microscope, a new world sprang to life under Sammie's eyes.

When Sammie and Bram arrived at Sammie's tall, mismatched house, she looked fiercely at him, daring him to say something about its peculiar appearance.

Bram's eyes traveled up the lavender edifice, his mouth opening as he stared. "It's like a purple castle," he said. "It's awesome!"

Sammie blinked at him. "Really?"

"I bet my mom would love this place," said Bram. "It's like art."

Like art. Sammie had never thought of it that way.

They walked right into her dad, who was fixing a broken piece of woodwork in the front hall.

"Um . . . hi, Dad. This is my new friend Bram. We're going upstairs to look at something." She began dragging Bram past him.

"Hey, wait!" said her dad, laughing. "Is that any way to treat your dad? Let me meet this Bram creature. He's not a bug or a squirrel, too, is he?"

"Daad," groaned Sammie.

To Sammie's frustration, Bram stopped and reached out a hand.

"Hi, Bram. I'm Dave," said Sammie's dad as they shook hands. "What are you two up to?"

"Sammie promised to show me her microscope."

Sammie's heart was in her throat. Did the two of them have to keep talking?

"Oh yeah? What are you going to look at?"

"Just some water from"—Sammie held her breath as Bram spoke—"near my house."

"We've really got to go, Dad," blurted Sammie, yanking at Bram's sleeve.

"Okay, okay," said her dad, flinging up his hands. "Don't let me get in the way."

They barreled up the steps, sneakers thumping. At the very top, they reached the door to the best room of the house: Sammie's Science Room.

She pushed open the door and, taking a deep breath, let Bram inside.

Sammie had convinced her parents to let her make their dusty attic her naturalist's studio. The attic was tinier than the floors below, jutting above their already tall, narrow house like a turret. Frosted skylights let in cloudy white light. Her dad had helped her add shelves to the walls and lug her desk up the stairs, but the rest of the setup was Sammie's brainchild.

She had modeled it on the old professor's house—his bookshelves, his cabinets of curios and specimens, the prints on his walls. Half the shelves were full of Sammie's naturalist books. The others held her personal museum—shells, feathers, fossils, plastic display boxes full of found insect husks and crab carapaces and fallen bird nests. On each box, she had carefully taped a neat handwritten label:

Seven-spot ladybug
Coccinella septempunctata
(Massachusetts State Insect!)
Found dead in the birdbath

On one wall, a poster listed every creature she'd ever found at the Field and the date she'd first seen it. And in a position of honor, on the desk set up by the window, stood her microscope.

She watched Bram, braced for criticism. But he said nothing, instead gazing raptly, gently fingering her specimens, reading her placards and posters. Then his gaze fell on the microscope.

"Whoa," he breathed. "That is one nice piece of equipment."

This was a real compliment coming from Bram, Sammie realized, given his love of gadgets.

In their jar, the hydra had vanished. Perhaps it had buried itself in the muck. Tiny brown dots still rushed about. Sammie set the jar gently beside the microscope. Picking up a plastic pipette, she dipped its point in the water, squeezed the bulb, and released. Brown and green bits swirled as pond water rushed up the neck of the pipette.

"Watch," she said to Bram as she dribbled two drops onto a slide. Her hands trembled with nervous excitement as she slid on a cover slip to just touch the mounded water's surface, then gently lowered it to flatten the water beneath it. She placed the slide on the microscope's stage and looked through the eyepieces. Then she turned the focus knob.

The dozens of specks grew into creatures. They jerked and darted. Some were larger than others. Some had long antennae; some had bars on their tiny clear bodies; some were long and thin, others perfectly round. Some had a brown speck inside, like a grain of wheat trapped in a marble.

"Let me see," said Bram.

"Okay," said Sammie, fascinated by the beings under her gaze. "Hang on."

It felt like that very first day when the old professor had

showed her the cells of a leaf, then the delicate structures of a dragonfly's wing, and, finally, cells he'd instructed Sammie to scrape with a toothpick from the inside of her own cheek.

A much larger creature dashed past the field of view. It had a long tail and a round body and two long antennae. "Whoa!" exclaimed Sammie. "What's *that*?"

"Let me *see*," squawked Bram, shifting from foot to foot.

She let him take her place. He took off his glasses to look down the scope. "You adjust the stage here, see." She guided his hand to the knob.

Bram crouched over the microscope, searching. He gasped. "Just look at that!" he exclaimed. "Wait! It's getting away! Quick!" He moved the stage. "Oh no, I went the wrong way." He shifted direction. Then he stared silently. "Wooow," he said. "That's the weirdest creature I've ever seen."

They dug out Sammie's copy of *Pond Life of the Eastern United States*. They decided the big fast creature was a copepod. They also identified diatoms and euglenas and a daphnia.

Bram's face was aglow with absorbed focus as he and Sammie pored through her books and traded places back and forth at the microscope, pursuing the identities of the elusive invertebrates. Bram asked her questions and seemed to be really listening to her opinions, his serious, concentrated frown resolving into pleased agreement with her as he pointed out why she was probably right. The two jostled gently against each other as they worked. Sammie paused at one point, taking in a deep breath of the dusty air in the carefully curated little room where she'd spent so many hours alone. She wasn't alone now, and it felt . . . nice.

WEATHER: Brisk, windy, partly cloudy
LOCATION: Muskrat Pond, The Field
TIME: 2:00 p.m.

Water collected by collecting
jar from old leaning
tree

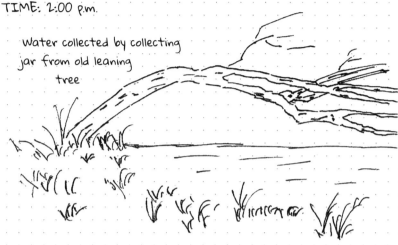

TIME: 4:00 p.m.
LOCATION: Home, Science Room - Microscope!

Inside collecting jar: many tiny brown specks. And the specks
are alive. They jerk and dart to and fro. None are bigger
than a grain of dust. Under the microscope:

diatom?   green   long plant   teardrop
                            structures: shaped
green ovals that   cell walls
twist and spiral as   tiny round
they swim-Euglena?   brown thing

A larger clear creature swims quickly by: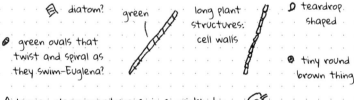

COPEPOD!

These are clear
like the others
and their innards
and structures
are visible

Passing by so fast it's hard to draw

10

THE STRANGE THING IN THE WOODS

When they'd identified as many creatures as they could on a dozen slides, Bram said, "What should we do with the rest of the jar? Pour it down the sink?"

"No way!" Sammie bristled. "There's a hydra in there. I'm not pouring it down the drain, or the other creatures, either."

Bram studied the jar critically. "Most invertebrates only live for a day or two anyway."

"We have to take them back to the Pond," Sammie insisted. She shook the water from the last microscope slide back into the jar mouth. She wanted those creatures to be safe, too. "'Take only pictures, leave only footsteps.' That's what I learned at the nature center where I used to live."

Bram tilted his head. "You don't 'take only pictures.' You've got this whole room full of specimens."

"That's different. Nothing I took was alive."

"It's still not what they said."

Sammie wished Bram wouldn't pick apart all her comments to point out the holes. The hydra was important, more important than some silly argument. Living creatures deserved to live out their lives in the wild. "I'm not pouring it down the sink," she repeated. She turned away so Bram wouldn't see she was upset. Maybe he really was just like any other boy.

But then she felt Bram's hand on her shoulder.

"Okay, okay," he said. "It's important to you. Look, I'm sorry I said that."

He was watching her through his round glasses with a gentle, careful gaze, like she was a wild animal he wanted to keep from running away. She swallowed and nodded.

He patted the jar. "We'll meet at the Field tomorrow," Bram declared, inviting himself back yet again, "and pour it in the Pond."

When they met at the boulder after school, Bram took the jar Sammie had hurried home to fetch and peered into it. "Have you seen the hydra?"

"No," admitted Sammie. Maybe it had already died, just like Bram had said.

Instead of an *I told you so* like Sammie expected, Bram's eyes widened dramatically. "I read about hydras on the internet last night," he said. "Scientists say they might be able to *live forever*."

"Oh, come on, Bram. Don't make fun of me," protested Sammie.

"No, I'm serious! They're more like a group of connected cells, a community, than a single creature. And the cells they're made of regenerate. Maybe for *thousands* of years."

"Weird!" Sammie shook the jar gently, searching for the tiny green creature.

Bram looked into the woods with anticipation. "Hey, I had an idea. Let's cut west through the entry woods and then south to get to the Pond, instead of walking down the Field path. I bet we could skip the alder grove. It'll make it faster."

Sammie hesitated. "We might get lost."

"This place is too small to get lost," argued Bram. "Besides, we can use the direction of the sun to get back out. I used to do orienteering at school."

"What's that?"

"Orienteering means navigating outdoors," said Bram. "You pay attention to the sun and the slope of the land. And my phone has a compass and a map." He pulled it out of his pocket and waved it around.

Sammie didn't have a phone of her own.

"My friends Matt and John used to be my orienteering

partners." Bram stared off into the distance, looking sad. "But I guess we'll never do that again."

An unfamiliar pang stung Sammie. Jealousy. Bram had friends in Seattle, maybe friends who were better than her. Friends who knew how to orienteer.

"Back home the forests go on forever and ever," mused Bram, wistful. "You really can get lost."

That cemented it. They'd go through the woods. Sammie wanted to show Bram that the forest here was great, too. "We'll have to figure out where to turn south to get to the Pond from this side." She lifted her chin and set off, turning right from the entry path.

The woodland here was populated mostly by deciduous trees. Tall oaks reached overhead, dappled light filtering through their young leaves. The bark and leaves made a tapestry of texture and color—some rough, some smooth, some dark, some mint-bright.

Underfoot, small shrubs dotted a forest floor papered by last year's leaves. The woods were loud with spring. Overhead, birds warbled and whistled their mating tunes. Sammie and Bram paused again and again to ID them. "A black-throated green warbler!" "Another black-and-white warbler!" A whole world reverberated above their heads.

Sammie peered a little farther into the woodland. "Hey, what's that?"

Fluttering neon colors interrupted the natural weave of silvery greens and browns.

They hiked closer. White string had been tied in large squares around the trees. Duct tape wrapped around the trunks marked off certain corners. Bram bent forward and examined one length of tape. "It says 'A,'" he said.

"And this one says 'B,'" said Sammie. "Weird."

They stared at the area of string and tape in silence. This was worrying, thought Sammie. Who had been coming here?

"Oh well." Bram dismissively swept his hand outward. "Let's get to the Pond. Look at the slope of the forest—this is where we have to turn."

As usual, Bram seemed ready to take charge. "This time we need to walk softly," said Sammie as a way of keeping a bit of control.

They crept noiselessly, footfalls silent on the damp soil of the valley bottom. When the Pond came into view, Sammie, in front, felt her breath stop. She brought her binoculars to her eyes. Bram needed no more to know she'd spotted something. She felt more than heard him lift his camera.

Cutting the water in a V shape was a small brown swimming animal. The water rippled out from around its nose. "The muskrat," Sammie whispered, so softly she wasn't sure Bram could even hear.

The muskrat hauled itself onto the bank, followed by two

little ones just like her but half her size. "Babies!" said Bram in a breathy squeal.

Water streamed from their thick, blackish-brown glistening coats. They looked like beavers but much smaller, the size of guinea pigs. And their tails weren't flat but long and thin, like a rat's.

The mother muskrat reached out and pulled a plant to her mouth with one tiny, four-fingered black hand, drawing it to yellowed teeth.

Bram's digital shutter clicked soft and fast.

Like hunters, they sneaked forward. They came nearer and nearer, until they hardly needed their equipment—so close that through her binoculars Sammie could count every whisker on the rodents' faces. Quickly Sammie sketched the little animals.

Then the adult muskrat raised her head. She lifted her nose up and down, testing the breeze. Muskrats, Sammie knew, can't see well but have expert senses of smell and hearing.

Then the mother shuffled rapidly forward and slid back into the water, closely followed by her youngsters. In three brown curves, they dove downward and vanished.

Sammie and Bram turned to each other with huge grins. "That was amazing!" burst out Sammie.

"I got terrific pictures!" Bram exclaimed.

Sammie raised her arms, basking in the glow of discovery. This was the largest mammal she'd spotted at the Field since a skunk had waddled by her last fall. And this animal had babies. The two little muskrats tucked close to their mother felt like a symbol—of her and of Bram, tucked into the landscape with all they needed right here.

Bram knelt by the water. "Here, let's pour out our jar." He unscrewed the lid. "Then we can head back up by the alder path. We got down here so fast, we still have time to birdwatch a little before you have to get home for your mom."

With a satisfied smile, he set off without waiting for her reply, underbrush crashing beneath his feet. "Good thing we came through the woods, huh?"

Sammie followed. In a mere moment, Bram had interrupted the warm feeling of camaraderie she'd felt. He seemed to care more about his smart idea and his great photos than about the muskrats themselves.

Back in the Field, the familiar landscape smelled of sunlight and dust and pollen. Sammie was pulled from her unhappy thoughts when a large orange-and-black butterfly fluttered past.

"Another monarch!" she exclaimed. The delicate creature circled them, then paused on the end of a reed, slowly opening and closing its patterned wings. "Look, it's visiting us."

The frail-looking butterfly wafted into the breeze like a torn shred of kite.

The butterfly and the hydra—both fit in here. Seemingly so fragile, they were survivors. Year after year, they could be found in just the right place: monarchs drinking from the meadow flowers; the hydra turning somersaults for thousands of years in the pond muck, sifting all the nourishment it needed from the water. They belonged, but their wildness made them free—no school, no parents and their rules, no crowded landscape of roads and buildings and cement.

Bram was bouncy and noisy and so very *human.* Sammie wanted to blend in, become like an animal or a bird or a butterfly herself. She wanted to *understand.* Could she do that, with Bram here? What would she lose if the Field were no longer a place just for her?

Bram's camera swung after the monarch and followed as it teetered away.

She pursed her lips in disapproval. "Your camera looks like a gun."

"It does?" Bram looked surprised. But also pleased. *Boys,* thought Sammie.

"I'm not shooting bullets, though," he added. "It takes a lot more brains to hunt with a camera than a gun. You've got to pick the aperture, the exposure, the shutter speed."

He got that wistful, faraway look in his eyes. "One time in Seattle," he went on, "I photographed an eagle grabbing a fish from the ocean. That was the best capture ever."

Sammie felt the unfamiliar pang again. She might not be sure she wanted to share the Field, but she didn't want Bram to like anywhere else better.

"Well, I prefer taking notes," she said. "That way I can describe what's going on."

"A picture is worth a thousand words," said Bram philosophically.

"It is not," said Sammie. "That's dumb."

But she didn't have a better comeback. Words flowed so easily in Sammie's notebook, but whenever Bram used his older-brother brainy voice, she always got tongue-tied.

She turned away and started heading back up the path toward home.

"Hey, come on, Sammie. You're always getting upset over some little thing," grumbled Bram.

"If you don't like hanging out with me, you don't have to," said Sammie.

Instead of the retort she expected, Bram caught up to her. "Are you kidding?" He bumped her playfully with his shoulder. "And miss the chance to see the muskrats and the pond invertebrates and all the other cool stuff you found?"

All the cool stuff *you* found. Maybe the things she was

sharing with Bram mattered to him—even as much as his own good ideas.

A little smile crept across her face, and she shrugged, trying to appear nonchalant. "Okay." She bumped him back. Then the two of them headed up the path together, Bram festively thwacking the tops of the grasses with his palms as they went.

WEATHER: Sunny, warm, no clouds
LOCATION: The Pond
TIME: 4:00 p.m.

MUSKRAT!
Swimming across
the Pond

and two babies!

Baby muskrats are
called "kits." Even after
they grow up, they stay
with their mothers
until the lodge gets
overcrowded

Eating pond weeds.
Muskrats also eat snails
and fish and salamanders

11
....

THE PACT

"It's one of *those days*," said Bram.

Sammie knew what he meant.

Some days the air crackled with life. Every bush and hollow rustled with the sound of wings and feet.

And then there were *those days*.

On *those days*, nothing moved or stirred. There never seemed to be a good reason for *those days*.

Bram and Sammie had been meeting nearly every day to explore. Sometimes he came to her house afterward, to use the microscope or set up the things they'd found—insect husks or sunbleached animal bones—in her museum. She'd introduced him to her mom. A couple times, Vicky had even come to pick up Bram and stayed for a cup of tea with Susan while the two kids finished what they were doing.

Susan seemed to like Vicky, their laughter filtering all the way up to the Science Room. And she tried but failed to contain her excitement that Sammie had made a friend. Sammie always rolled her eyes when her mom got enthusiastic—she was too proud to admit that her mom had been right about needing companionship. To her surprise, though, she found herself looking forward to seeing Bram in the Field, waiting for her on his favorite boulder.

She started spotting him at school, too—when Bram's recess was ending and Sammie's just starting. Sometimes they talked about what they might see that day in the Field. It lit the otherwise lonely playground with a glow of anticipation.

Now, though, the grasses of the Field stood motionless. Not a whisper of air rustled their stems.

"Maybe it's too hot," said Sammie, deflated.

And it was hot, crushingly so—the first truly hot day now that June had arrived.

"You know where we haven't gone?" said Bram.

"We go everywhere except the Junkyard House."

"No, we've never passed the stone wall into the forest at the bottom of the Field," said Bram.

"Oh," said Sammie. "I don't really think of that as the Field anymore. I never go there."

"Why not? It's all connected. I bet it's cooler."

Sammie had gone beyond the stone wall only once. The forest there was shadowy and forbidding. Unlike the grassland, woods seemed threatening—she couldn't see around each bend, so she couldn't tell if anyone might be coming. And the path dead-ended before too long at hectic Split Road, rushing with cars. She hadn't stayed long, jogging back even more quickly than she'd come.

Thick woods normally didn't have as many birds in them anyway. Birds and animals preferred edges and borders between habitats. They liked to hunt for food where it was easy to see, in the open, but near where they could hide if necessary.

Still, she reminded herself, it was just woodland, nature itself. And besides, she didn't have to be alone this time— Bram was here.

"Sure," she said, more casually than she felt.

At the bottom of the Field, the trees loomed, silent, guarding a darkness. The trees here were big—even bigger than the ones in the fringe of woods at the entry path.

Now a breeze wafted out, beckoning Sammie and Bram into deep shade. They stepped into the stillness.

Some trees here had deep, sweeping boughs of feathery needles. They were hemlocks. Above the hemlocks grew larger trees with stout trunks whose branches only started way up high. Long thin needles poked in clusters from the high boughs. Pine trees.

"It's so quiet," murmured Bram. The only sound was of softly crunching needles underfoot.

The arched trees overhead made a dome. The trunks formed pillars. The path stretched like a central aisle. The woods no longer felt threatening but solemn.

"It's like a cathedral," murmured Sammie. "Let's lie on our backs and look up."

They did, their chests rising and falling as they gazed reverently into the layers of green. A sweet pine smell seeped from the forest floor.

Then the silence was broken.

"KUK-KUK-KUK-KUK-KUK-KUK-KUK-KUK!"

Sammie sucked in a breath. "Don't move," whispered Bram.

"KUK-KUK-KUK-KUK-KUK-KUK-KUK-KUK!" The ringing call sang out again. And then a shape followed, arrowing through the air of the tree canopy above their heads. For an instant, Sammie saw the bird in flight, like some prehistoric creature, a small pterodactyl with a long, pointed face and broad wings. Then with a loud thump, it landed on the side of a dead tree.

Silently, Sammie brought her binoculars to her eyes. Bram lifted his long-lensed camera. She could hear his soft digital shutter again and again: *Schlik-schlik-schlik-schlik.*

Above them clung a woodpecker as long as Sammie's forearm. Its black beak was as thick and long as her finger. On its head, it sported a bright red crest like a pirate's bandanna. Its cheeks and neck were striped black and white, and it had a red mustache. Its strong, chunky body was black.

"It's a pileated woodpecker," whispered Bram, his voice awed.

"I've never seen one," Sammie murmured back. "Just in the bird guide."

The woodpecker descended the tree trunk with jerky, short movements, like a mechanical toy. Then with its powerful bill, it began hammering at the tree. Chips of wood flew out to either side. The pounding rang over the woodland.

They lay spellbound until the bird turned its big head outward to stare into the forest. Then it launched itself and in big, dipping arcs flew over their heads and disappeared among the trees.

"I can't believe it," said Bram. "That's only my second pileated ever!"

Sammie felt ready to burst with happiness. She felt, all at once, that she wanted to say something, do something, to make the moment complete. Rising slowly, she lifted her arms in the direction the bird had gone.

"Let's make a pact, Bram," she said impulsively. "That the Field will be our special place, and we'll keep it our secret, just you and me."

Bram's eyes glowed at her. "I like that," he said. "I've

never had a secret place before. Just the cabin, but that was my whole family's."

He stood beside her and raised his arms, too. Then he lowered them again.

"We should give this place a better name," he said. "It's so much more than just 'the Field.' It's got woods and a pond and maybe things we haven't even found yet."

Sammie hesitated. "I've always called it the Field."

"Don't you think it would make our spot extra special, to have a name we chose together?" Bram said.

Sammie closed her eyes and knitted her brows. Against her reddish inner lids, she pictured the pileated winging across blue patches of sky between the trees. She thought of the waving grasses of her favorite part of this landscape, the *Field* itself. And then, unbidden, into her imagination floated one of the huge monarchs they'd seen already so many times, bright wings catching the breeze.

"I *do* have an idea," she said. She opened her eyes.

"Oh yeah?" Bram was looking at her hopefully, a warm shine of affection on his face. The edges of his glasses reflected the pines and made him look a little like a forest creature himself.

"Winghaven," said Sammie. "We could call it Winghaven. It's a safe place, so it's a haven, for woodpeckers and for butterflies and for muskrats and for us. And it's full of wings, and wings make things free."

"Sammie, that's *perfect*." Bram lifted his arms again. "We belong to you, Winghaven," he said.

At first reluctantly, but with a growing sense that it was something she needed to do, she raised her arms, too, tugged by the sense of ceremony, by the slender needle of the pileated woodpecker stitching all of them together with invisible thread.

"Yes," she said. "Winghaven, we belong to you." Something tightly held seemed to uncurl in her chest.

12

PETE

On Saturdays, when Bram took his violin lessons, Sammie went to Winghaven by herself. The Field—Winghaven now—held a special silence when she came here alone. In the quiet, the wind spoke differently. It stole over the tops of the weeds, rustling them softly, and sent whispers through the trees.

But Sammie felt restless and unsettled. In two weeks, the school year would end, and she'd be packed off to camp every day. Maybe she'd done the wrong thing, renaming her Field.

She'd planned to work on her plant collection in the meadow today, but instead she turned toward the entry woods. She was thinking about all that tape and string she and Bram had seen down there. She wished she knew what it was about. It made her worried.

She hiked briskly along the same woodland route she and Bram had followed. Before long, she arrived at the spot near the bottom of the slope. There was the tape, and there was the string. But there between them now—white things. She craned her neck. They looked like . . . laundry baskets?

Really?

She hiked over to take a closer look.

They *were* laundry baskets, the plastic kind. Rough holes had been punched into the bottoms. And each was labeled, in black permanent marker, with a number—as well as the name of the university where her dad worked.

It was creepy to think someone else was using these woods for a mysterious purpose.

She took a good look around. These woods were open and airy, and no one could sneak up on her. She'd never collected plants in the woods—maybe she could learn something new to impress Bram with later.

Settling down, she unpacked her notebook and plant-collecting materials: several flat cardboard sheets held together by rubber bands to store leaves and flowers. She never took whole plants but chose a few sample leaves and blossoms from each one. At home, she would put them under heavy books until they were pressed and dried, then glue them into her plant notebook.

So deeply was she focused on her task that the noise of footsteps caught her by surprise. And the steps sounded funny: *thump-swish*, *thump-swish*, a dragging rustle.

She grabbed her pack and collection and looked around desperately for a hiding spot. Just upslope, the broken crown of a tumbled tree made a thicket of dead leaves. Swiftly and silently, she went over to it and shrank like a groundhog behind its cloaking brush.

Between the trees, a figure came into view.

A grown-up, but he looked younger than Sammie's parents. He was tall and lanky with blondish hair that stuck upward in every direction. But where Sammie's hair was bright yellow gold, his hair was sand-colored and as unkempt as if he'd never brushed it. He wore an army-green vest with lots of pockets and a short-sleeved plaid shirt. His jeans looked like blue drinking straws on his long legs. One leg ended in a cast. His footsteps had sounded strange because he was on crutches.

And across his vest he wore a black strap ending in a dark object.

Binoculars.

Raising them to his eyes, he looked up into the trees, then pulled a yellow notebook out of his vest pocket and jotted a few notes.

Was he bird-watching? And taking notes, like her? Automatically Sammie's hand reached back to her pack to touch the spine of her notebook. But her heart caught in her throat as she felt empty space. Her notebook wasn't there. She scanned the woodland floor, but it was nowhere to be seen.

The man tucked away his notebook. From another vest pocket, he took out a flat metal object. It looked like the kitchen scale Sammie's mom used to weigh flour.

Shuffling laboriously about, he set the little metal plate on the forest floor and carefully balanced each laundry basket atop it—they seemed too big for such a little scale, but he looked satisfied. Then he fished out a second notebook, green this time, from one of his pockets that seemed bottomless. He wrote something down.

This didn't look like bird-watching at all. Or like laundry, for that matter.

He stacked the laundry baskets. Now he began untying the markers from the trees. Each time he undid a piece of flagging or string, he pulled out a roll of the same color, already a tangle of previously knotted lengths, and tied it on, as if trying not to waste anything.

A warbler twittered a bright song above Sammie's head. The man glanced up, lifting his binoculars, and scribbled quickly in his yellow notebook. Sammie scrunched deeper into her hiding spot. Then something on the forest floor not too far from her caught his attention.

He swung forward with surprising grace despite his crutches and picked up Sammie's notebook from among the leaves.

Oh no. Sammie's fingernails dug into her palms. He turned the pages with great attention.

"Huh!" he said aloud.

He scanned the area, sandy eyebrows creased. Sammie tried to stay absolutely still and invisible. *Please, please, put it down,* she thought. *Please put it down and go away.*

Instead, he braced the notebook between his arm and one crutch and turned to shuffle away. He was taking it!

Sammie leaped to her feet. "Wait!" she shouted. "That's mine!"

The young man startled, leaping sideways to hide behind a tree. The movement might've been graceful if he hadn't been wearing a cast.

Instead, he crashed to the ground in a crunching of leaves and shrubs.

"Ouch," he said, sitting up and ruefully rubbing his cast. He spotted Sammie standing in the middle of the brush of her own hiding place and lifted both eyebrows.

"Huh," he said again.

"Sorry," said Sammie. She felt badly now for surprising him.

"It's okay," he said. "I should've known better."

"That's my notebook," said Sammie.

The young man had dropped it in his fall. He picked it up. "*You* made this?"

"Yes," said Sammie. "Please put it back."

"I thought someone had forgotten it." He hauled himself to his feet, long limbs unfolding like one of Bram's construction toys, and shuffled the few steps to exactly where he'd found it. He placed it down with big hands, more delicately this time, like handling an egg. Then he smiled at her. His whole face crinkled up when he did that. "What's your name?"

"I'm not supposed to talk to strangers."

He had a funny face, especially when his eyebrows went up like that. It was long and doglike and uneven, with a thin nose ending in a round knob, and drooping eyelids. It would have been a sad face, except that the creases around his eyes showed how frequently he smiled, and his mouth had a slight upturn, as if controlling a laugh.

"Ah, of course," he said. His mouth quirked sideways, a look of mingled regret and understanding. He picked up his fallen crutches and resettled their ends on the forest floor. "I'll leave you alone."

"Wait," Sammie blurted out, curiosity getting the better of her. He was on crutches and couldn't chase her. At a moment's notice, she could flee back up through the woodland and escape. "What are you doing?"

The man glanced around and sat on a fallen log. Perhaps he needed to rest, or maybe he wanted to make himself look less threatening. It worked. He looked smaller like that.

"I'm a graduate student," he said. "I'm finishing up an insect study for a lab at the university."

A scientist.

"With laundry baskets?" she said a little incredulously.

He grinned a big, lopsided toothy smile. "Those are to measure leaf litter," he said. "We're trying to learn if leaf fall affects insect numbers. Outdoors, everything is connected."

That last sentence sounded like the naturalists she used to talk to at the nature center.

"I thought the string might be from people coming to cut the trees down," said Sammie.

"Fortunately not!" He laughed. "I mark off study plots and count insects in a grid inside."

"How come you have binoculars?"

"The little investigator is full of questions," he said, smiling. "I got into studying bugs because they're food for birds. I'm also birding. And taking notes, like you."

He held up his small yellow notebook.

Sammie nibbled her lip. "Can . . . can I see?"

"I guess that's a fair trade," he said in his slow thoughtful voice. "Here."

He tossed the yellow notebook toward her, spine first. It fluttered across the forest floor and fell in front of her hiding place.

Sammie stuck her arm through the branches and picked it up.

Its cover was made of a flexible material, bent from being rolled up in a vest pocket. The spine was string-bound. Printed on the cover: WATERPROOF NOTEBOOK. Underneath, there was a handwritten name: Pete Welch.

Inside, it looked nothing like hers, either. Pete's notebook was a list of numbers and letters:

1625	*GCFL song only*
1629	*RBNU (x2)*
	BGGN
	HETH
1638	*HOWR*

"What does it mean?" said Sammie.

Pete grinned, looking pleased. "The numbers are twenty-four-hour time. After noon, instead of starting over at one p.m., you keep counting, thirteen hours, fourteen hours, until twenty-four hours at midnight. So sixteen twenty-five means four twenty-five p.m."

"Weird," said Sammie.

"The letters are birds."

"I don't get it."

"H-O-W-R, for example. H-O for house and W-R for wren.

So it's short for house wren. I saw one today." He smiled as understanding dawned on her face. "It's a great way to quickly survey birds."

"How come you're surveying birds?" asked Sammie.

"It's not an official survey. I'm working on a project of my own." He tilted a conspiratorial smile at her.

"What kind of project?" asked Sammie, wide-eyed.

"Every year the Audubon Society does their Christmas Bird Count," said Pete. "They're a nonprofit group that tries to protect birds. The birder who finds the most species that day wins. Some people call competitions like that a 'Big Day.' All year, I keep track of how diverse the spots in my region are. That way I know the best places to go when the count rolls around. Last year I almost won, but I birded a different area. This year, I'm thinking of switching to this side of town. Of course, then I broke my ankle in a groundhog hole, and it's slowing my birding down." He gingerly waved his foot.

"That's too bad," said Sammie.

"It's healing up," said Pete with an easy shrug.

"This place is awesome for birds," said Sammie. "The best." Pride overtook caution. "The grassy part where I go has the most, though." She gestured backward toward the Field.

"You certainly know a lot about it," Pete said. "You've got quite the notebook."

"It's not as scientific as yours," she said.

She wondered if he thought her notebook was silly. Her sketches that Bram still insisted on correcting. The little poems she sometimes wrote.

"On the contrary," said Pete. "It's amazing. How did you learn to do that?"

Sammie's heart lifted.

"The nature center where I used to live had a book about nature journaling," she said. "I decided to try it."

"You're very observant, kiddo," said Pete.

"My friend Bram helped me some with the drawings," she admitted. "He's a nature photographer."

"A nature photographer. Will wonders never cease?" Pete smiled. "Is he your age?"

"He's a year older." Sammie felt a little jealous of Pete's interest in Bram. She burst out defensively, "I like coming here by myself better."

"Oh? How come?"

"It's more like a real scientist to do things on my own."

Pete eyed her thoughtfully. "Come now," he said. "That's not true."

"Sure it is," said Sammie. "Like Jane Goodall. She was always by herself."

She'd read how Jane Goodall had gone alone into the African jungle, patiently seeking the chimpanzees she had come to study. Finally, she'd convinced the great apes to trust her. They let her touch them, share their food, even hold their babies. She'd become like one of them.

"Ah, Jane Goodall." Pete's ready smile broadened across his face in a look of admiration. "Goodall didn't work completely alone, you know. She spent a lot of time in the jungle by herself, it's true. But she had a scientific adviser, Louis Leakey, who reviewed her findings. And when she first moved to Tanzania from England to do her work, her mom came with her to keep house and help her adjust."

"Seriously?" exclaimed Sammie. "My mom's too busy these days to help me nature watch."

"Each person has their strengths. You should look for and value the people who share your passions. Scientists need collaborators."

Sammie considered his words, her brows knitted.

Pete lifted his foot, awkwardly waving his cast. "I'd better set off," he said. "Takes me longer to get home with this thing."

Sammie found herself wishing Pete would stay, with his gawky, thoughtful smile and his long nose and his crooked teeth and his notebooks and all the things he knew. A real scientist—like the biologist who had given her the microscope. She felt too shy to say anything, though.

"Happy birding, kid," Pete said. "And your friend Bram,

too. You're lucky to have a friend like that." He hauled himself to his feet and stuck his crutches under his arms.

Sammie felt a pang of guilt for complaining.

Pete swung back over the creek toward his pile of laundry baskets. Sammie had only just time to wonder how he would carry them before he hooked them over his forehead like an overgrown turtle. Then he stumped away into the forest.

Sammie waited to move until Pete disappeared. Then she realized in consternation that his notebook was still in her lap. Should she chase after him? Should she leave it for him to find?

She would hold on to it and try to give it back another day, she decided. Maybe he'd come looking for it next Saturday, and she'd get to see him again.

WEATHER: Sunny, hot
LOCATION: Woods, entrance of The Field
TIME: 3:30 p.m.

Green fronds
Spilling over the ground saying
This spot
Is sacred
To me.

Like a flag
It waves its leaves
Showing that it
Is queen
Of that spot in the forest.

CANADA
MAYFLOWER
common all
over the
woods

A day passes.
New sprouts appear
The fern grows
It now covers
A four-foot space—
It is beautiful.

Years pass.
The fern grows old.
Slowly it withers
It gives one more
   burst of strength
Then dies.

It has given
Its body to the soil
The ground grows rich and fertile.
And still its soul lingers

Saying that it
Is still queen
Of that spot in the forest.

13

TROUBLES

School was winding down, and Sammie's teacher was letting the class do more independent work. Sammie had finished her assignments and used the time to research the creatures of Winghaven.

Loss of milkweed lands monarchs on endangered list—she read the headline on her assigned school laptop.

Did all the news about nature have to be bad?

She read that monarch caterpillars ate only milkweed. Each summer, monarchs migrated north into the United States to lay their eggs on these plants so their larvae would have food to eat when they hatched. Without large meadows of milkweed, the butterflies wouldn't reproduce.

Most troubling for the monarch, the use of herbicides on farm crops has led to a decline in milkweed, said the article. *Monarch butterfly populations have fallen 80 percent within three decades.*

Sammie shut her eyes. In her mind danced the image of the handsome orange-and-black butterflies among the grasses of Winghaven.

Winghaven still had monarchs. And milkweed, too. At the end of last summer, she'd loved seeing the big milkweed seedpods. As long as her palm and shaped like a skinny football, they began to split while still green. As the pods dried and turned brown, they broke fully open, spilling fluffy white stuff that, on closer look, carried seeds: flat, dark brown, and paper-thin, each attached to a white parachute, like a dandelion seed but bigger. Autumn breezes floated them across Winghaven until the air sparkled with tufts.

She pulled up a map of her town on her laptop and was soon zooming in on the big blank green space where she spent so many hours.

"What are you doing?" came a voice from behind her.

Robert.

Sammie frantically put a hand over her browser window. "None of your business."

He tried to peer past her hand. She leaned away from his spiky black hair and broad shoulders without taking her palm from the screen.

"I bet Sammie's got an online boyfriend," he taunted.

Sammie reddened. "I do not!"

"Then what's so secret? Hey, everyone," he started to shout, "Sammie's—"

"Shut up, Robert!" She smacked his hand.

"Ow," howled Robert, grabbing his hand. "That *hurts*, ow, ow!" Sammie stared. Had she really hurt him? Abruptly he let go of it. "Actually, no, you hit like a baby."

"I do not."

"You do too."

"Do NOT."

"Robert and Sammie, I asked you to leave each other alone." The teacher's voice cut across the room.

"Sammie hit me."

"Sammie, I've told you to control your temper." Mrs. Gladwell glared at them.

"Sorry." Sammie turned back to the screen, upset at getting in trouble. She quickly minimized her browser. The moment Mrs. Gladwell looked away, Robert leaned forward again.

"Online boyfriend," he whispered. "If you don't show me, that's what I'll tell everyone."

Sammie's chest tightened in panic. Then she had a brainstorm.

"I'm just looking for something else to do this summer. My mom wants to send me to stupid day camp." It was kind of the truth, after all.

"What, you're too good for Camp Shriver?" said Robert. "What's wrong with it?"

"How did you know I meant there?"

"That's where everybody goes. My dad makes me go every year."

"*You're* going to Camp Shriver? Oh no!" burst out Sammie without thinking. "That's the worst news ever!"

"The worst ever, huh?" sneered Robert. "Jeez. Well, Little Miss Perfect, it's not like anyone wants *you* around all summer, either! Did you think about that?"

If she hadn't known better, Sammie almost would've thought Robert sounded hurt. But she did know better.

"Sammie, come here," said Mrs. Gladwell.

Sammie's heart sank. She slowly got up and shuffled to her teacher's desk.

Mrs. Gladwell looked her over. "I know Robert can be hard to deal with."

Sammie swallowed past the lump in her throat.

"He's got some troubles, Sammie, but he mostly bothers you because he wants your attention," said Mrs. Gladwell. "Keeping your cool will help. You're a smart kid—don't let your emotions run away with your head."

Sammie felt a surge of frustration. That wasn't it. Robert didn't like her at all. He just enjoyed cutting her down. Why was Mrs. Gladwell yelling at her and not him?

"Okay," she said.

"I'm going to keep an eye on Robert, all right?" said her teacher. "Now go on back to work."

Sammie turned toward her desk. There stood Robert—still. He was staring down at her computer, which she'd left open.

"Hey!" she exclaimed, hurrying but trying not to attract Mrs. Gladwell's attention. "Get away. That's mine."

"Is it against the law to stand here?" said Robert. "If it's yours, it's probably boring." He sauntered away.

Sammie hastily sat down at her computer. Nothing looked any different. Good thing she'd minimized that browser window.

14
TAKING RISKS

That afternoon, Sammie lay flat on her stomach on the Hillock beside Bram, morosely twiddling a thread of grass between her fingers. Her binoculars lay unused on the gravel beside her.

Bram glanced at her.

"Is something wrong?" he said.

Lots of things felt wrong, thought Sammie.

It was almost time for camp to start. Deep in her pack, she had Pete's notebook hidden away. Something was stopping her from telling Bram about him. Pete, and all the things he'd told her about science, felt like one thing she could keep for herself while Bram got to be here all summer long without her. Pete had said he was finishing up his study, so chances were he wouldn't be around much. And even if Bram did run into Pete, he wouldn't talk to him. Bram had promised to keep this place just his and Sammie's.

Just his and Sammie's. Maybe she shouldn't have talked so much to Pete, either, she thought guiltily. But she'd had to—Pete had found her notebook. Besides, Pete had just felt *right*, as part of this place as a forest animal.

Probably she'd never see Pete again. So it wouldn't matter. She pushed her niggling worries deep into the back of her brain.

"I start camp after school ends," she said, muffling her voice in her arms.

"Oh," said Bram. "Right."

"I'm going to hate it."

Unlike her mom, Bram did her the favor of not trying to convince her otherwise. He didn't say he was sad she wouldn't be around, though. He simply studied the long grasses waving under the June sun. Sammie burrowed deeper into her arms, inhaling the dusty scent of soil below her nose.

"Hey," he said after a while. "I have an idea."

"Yeah?"

"Why don't you tell your mom you can hang out at my place this summer? She's only putting you in camp so you won't be alone, right? Well, if you're with us, you definitely won't be alone."

Sammie rolled over. Could that possibly work? She felt a stirring of hope. "I could really tell her that?"

"Sure! My mom can watch both of us. She knows I come here anyway, 'cause I told her about it before I met you. And then I won't be so lonely all the time."

Lonely. Bram said he felt lonely. And he wanted to spend his whole summer here with just her. As a few fluffy clouds sailed past in the depthless blue sky above Bram's head, a warm feeling stole over Sammie.

"What if your mom tells my mom about Winghaven, though? They talk a lot these days."

Vicky still seemed exotic and intimidating to Sammie, with her art and her paint-stained clothes and long black hair. Yet whenever Vicky stopped by Sammie's house, Sammie's mom always seemed perfectly at ease. In fact, it was Vicky who looked to Susan for advice, asking all about the town, the schools, the other kids, and the teachers.

"Oh, nah, she won't even think of it," said Bram.

"My mom will be furious if she finds out I've been hiding it from her all this time. What if she tells me I can't come here anymore?"

"If you never take risks, you'll never get what you want," said Bram. "You can't hide stuff forever, Sammie. You keep too many secrets."

If a bird couldn't keep a secret, Sammie thought, *she'd lose her eggs.*

"One of these days, maybe you should just be yourself and tell her the truth," said Bram.

The thought sent a shiver of fear down Sammie's spine.

Still. Suppose she really could stay here this summer? She remembered Pete—what he'd said about having a scientific collaborator. Maybe Bram could be like that for her. They could learn everything about this place. Bram could record it in his photos, and she in her notebooks, like the naturalists of long ago. Maybe someday someone would read her writings and marvel at how much they had learned and seen. Just like Pete with her notebook.

As if answering her thought, Bram spoke again. "We could come up with a summer project to do together. Something actually scientific. Right now, all we do is watch nature."

"Well, I write things down," said Sammie. "And you take pictures."

"Right, but we could do something really big," said Bram.

This sounded like another of Bram's take-charge ideas. "What kind of big?" she asked.

Bram gnawed at his bottom lip. "I don't know yet. I could ask my dad for help. He's good at coming up with scientific ideas."

"We promised not to share Winghaven."

The Pete guilt niggled at Sammie again.

"Well, I didn't mean we would share. It's *our* place, don't worry." Bram socked her gently on the shoulder. "It's not like my dad's going to come here."

"I bet we can come up with something on our own." Sammie's pride awoke. "Maybe we can use all the notes and pictures we already have. Something to show how it's all connected. To show how important Winghaven really is."

"Exactly!" said Bram. "But first you've got to talk to your mom."

Sammie squeezed her hands into fists and stretched her limbs all the way out on the gravelly soil. "Okay, I'll ask!" she said. "Oh, *please* let her say yes."

"She will. I know it." Bram leaped to his feet and reached out both hands to help Sammie up. "Let me ask my mom first. You'll see. This is going to be the best summer ever."

Bram beamed one of the biggest smiles she'd ever seen on his face. Then he turned to the sunlit expanses of Winghaven, the sun brightening his face under his dark shell of hair. "Let's bird-watch awhile and see if we come up with any great ideas."

As she trailed after Bram down the path, Sammie's thoughts were crowded with worries. What if Vicky said no? What if her mom found out about Winghaven? Bram said she kept too many secrets. Now she wished she had told him about Pete, but it felt too late. He was already charging ahead through the grasses. What if he got upset that she'd been hiding something and took back his offer of letting her stay at his place this summer?

Deep in her thoughts, she followed Bram halfway into the brush before she stopped. "We can't go that way, remember? That slope leads to the Junkyard House."

Bram gazed speculatively. "I've never seen it."

Sammie grimaced. "It's nothing special. Just a house and a bunch of junk."

"I want to look." Bram crept forward. Sammie tailed him reluctantly, trying to make as little noise as possible.

They edged through saplings and brush until the Junkyard House hove into view like a tattered pirate ship.

The white paint was peeling, showing patches of bare wood. The doors and windowsills had probably once been painted red but had faded to mottled pinkish gray. One broken window sash leaned awry. The windows themselves were black flags against the walls.

In the yard stood the broken-down cars and heaps of scrap metal. Patches of bare soil and stains that looked like oil were interspersed amid the scrubby grass.

"Okay," whispered Sammie. "You've seen it. Can we go now?"

"Hang on," said Bram. "What's that?" He kept moving forward.

"Bram," whispered Sammie urgently. "Stop! I don't want to go in there!"

"I think it's a for sale sign." Bram sneaked fully into the yard, lifting his camera to his eyes as he went. "Lookit!"

The air was split at that moment by a deep, furious barking, startling Sammie and Bram half out of their skin. They leaped backward. Bram crashed into Sammie, who fell over. She scrambled to her feet, and they both tore back up the slope, racing through the brush until they reached the path again.

Bram flung himself down, laughing and panting. "Stupid!" he exclaimed. "That dog was inside. You could tell by how muffled the barking was."

"Yeah, but the people might have come out to find us!" Sammie sucked on her arm. A thin branch had slapped her and left a stinging red cut.

"Nah," said Bram. "Most people are at work now. I bet they're not even home."

"I guess." Sammie's heart was hammering. "Anyway, let's not do that again."

Bram wasn't really listening. He had turned his camera screen upward. It beeped softly as he opened the most recent photo.

"It *was* a for sale sign," he said. "Look."

Sammie peered over his shoulder. "Maybe if new people

move in, they'll be less creepy and not keep all that trash in their yard," she said.

"Maybe," said Bram.

"I hope whoever it is leaves us alone."

"I bet that ugly old house will be hard to sell," Bram said. "Probably nothing will change."

15

BROKEN PROMISES

Sammie's first thought the next morning was to wonder what Vicky had decided. But a downpour meant indoor recess, so Sammie didn't see Bram. As she trudged home from the bus stop in the rain, she worried Bram wouldn't be at Winghaven, either.

But at last, as if in answer to her wishes, the rain began to die away. Not waiting for the drizzle to completely stop, Sammie jumped on her bicycle. Instead of softly stealing down Winghaven's entry path as usual, she ran. Soil splashed up around her sneakers.

There, on his usual boulder, sat Bram. He'd made it. "Well?" gasped Sammie, the little blond curls that always formed at her hairline in wet weather sticking to her forehead. She wiped them back.

Bram was dry as a bone, sitting primly on a raincoat. "Well, what?"

Sammie could hardly believe Bram wasn't thinking about something so important. "Well, what did your mom say? Can I stay with you this summer?"

"Oh, that," said Bram. He scrunched up his nose.

Sammie felt herself slowly freezing into a cold, unhappy, rainy lump.

"I couldn't ask yet," said Bram. "She had a sale of a big painting fall through and has been in a crummy mood. I decided to wait until she feels better."

"I was afraid you were going to say she'd said no."

"Nah. She's going to say yes." He jumped up and socked her on the shoulder. "Don't be a worrywart." His dark eyes rested on her with warm affection. "Let's go see what comes out after the rain."

They headed down into Winghaven, binoculars and camera at the ready.

Then they rounded the bend.

In the middle of the path sat a shape: lanky, cross-legged, straight-backed, almost tall enough even sitting down to be visible over the Winghaven grasses, sand-colored hair mingling with their gold and green hues.

"Hi again, Sammie," said Pete, smiling. "You were right about this place. It's amazing for birds."

Sammie felt her skin prickle as she flushed to the roots of her hair. Now Bram knew that she'd met Pete.

"I'm sure glad to see you again, kid," Pete added. He looked as much a part of this landscape as he had when she'd met him, in sturdy dark green rain gear from head to toe, hair slicked down like a wet dog. "You didn't happen to find my notebook, did you? I realized I'd lost it when I got home."

Slowly Sammie reached back and drew his notebook from her pack. Bram watched her every move.

"I thought it might be gone for good!" Pete said. "I should've known the little investigator would have it."

In spite of herself, Sammie felt herself warmed by Pete's big, kind smile and compliments. He just had a way of making her feel important.

"Sammie, I have to go home." Bram grabbed her sleeve. "And you're coming, too." He pulled her forcibly back up the path. They rounded the bend, out of Pete's sight.

"Hey!" protested Sammie, shaking off his grasp. "Let go, Bram."

Bram stumped off. She hesitated, then chased him back up to the entry woods. He turned to her, scowling.

"Who the heck was *that*?"

Sammie reddened again. "He's the person who had all that string and tape down by the creek." Briefly she described her encounter with Pete a few days before. Maybe she could convince Bram that she'd just *had* to talk to Pete.

And as she talked, her guilt faded and her enthusiasm grew. She told Bram about Pete's insect study and how he kept his bird notes. She told him about Pete's plans for the Big Day.

"He keeps track of things differently than we do—no photos, no drawings," said Sammie. As her words tumbled out, she realized it might even be fun to share Pete with Bram. She tried harder. "He knew a whole lot about nature. I thought . . . I thought it might be nice if he started showing up to teach us some things. Both of us."

Bram gave a short grunt, staring off into the trees.

Finally, Sammie trailed off. "Why aren't you saying anything?" she faltered.

"Why didn't you tell me?" said Bram.

"I . . . I don't know." Sammie turned pink. "I just . . . I forgot." Her words fell like concrete onto the wet path.

"You forgot!" Bram snorted. "Right. *We promised not to share Winghaven,*' you said." His usual easy good humor had vanished, and his dark brows were drawn together. "I guess that just means me."

"But Pete's different," protested Sammie. She felt terrible, but she tried to push it down. Maybe she could make Bram understand. "I didn't bring him—he was already here. And he had binoculars. He's a birder."

"We made a pact!" said Bram. He looked furious.

"Bram, please just wait. Pete's a scientist, for real," she

said. She just had a good feeling about Pete. Bram would surely like him once he stopped being angry at her. "Like your dad, but about nature. Maybe he knows things about the Field—I mean, Winghaven—that we don't know."

"Then it's probably not worth knowing," snapped Bram.

"He has a whole notebook full of birds he's seen. He really cares about them—as much as we do."

"How do you know? You only just met him."

"Just a feeling! I liked him."

"Yeah, I noticed," said Bram. "We were going to come up with an idea ourselves!"

"Well, we still can!" protested Sammie weakly.

"I thought this place was going to be special," said Bram. "Our place, yours and mine! I guess your mom's not the only person you don't tell the truth to."

And now that Bram had said the thing she felt most guilty about, Sammie felt a surge of anger mask her regret. "Well, it used to be *my* place," she shouted. "But I let you come here!"

"You don't own it!" said Bram. "I can come here any time I want!"

"Why can't you just try and understand?" Sammie's throat tightened. "You always have to take charge and be the best at everything. We could've learned something from Pete, but now you were so rude that we'll probably never see him again!" She crossed her arms and turned away so Bram wouldn't see she was about to cry.

"Oh, it's all my fault, then," said Bram angrily. "I'm going home."

Sammie clung stubbornly to her fit of temper. Bram was being unfair, she told herself. He'd see things her way eventually. He'd always been the one to give in before.

Instead, he stormed off up the path.

"Look," Sammie finally burst out, "I'm sorry!"

But Bram was already too far away to hear.

16
PLAYGROUND DISASTERS

Sammie felt even crummier than usual at school the next day. She couldn't concentrate on anything Mrs. Gladwell said.

Why, she thought as she and the class turned a page in their English book, *does everything have to go so slowly?* It gave her too much time to think about Bram and how she'd ruined any chance of spending the summer with him at Winghaven.

She would find Bram at recess and say it was her fault, she decided at last. He could have been nicer, but she'd broken their pact.

At lunchtime Sammie sprang from her seat. She ate fast, then waited for the cafeteria's big double doors to open. On the playground's asphalt, she spotted the line of sixth graders from Period 1 recess about to go back inside.

She searched out his bowl of dark brown hair, his T-shirt and jeans.

"Bram!" He lifted his head as she hurried up to him. "Bram, I want to tell you—" she blurted out.

"Sammie *does* have a boyfriend!" Robert's shout broke into her hasty speech. She whipped her head around. There he was, sauntering forward with his stocky shoulders and mean-looking jutting face.

"Yeah, she's flirting with the boys from *sixth* grade!" That was Mark, playing sidekick again.

"Shut up!" shouted Sammie. She turned back toward Bram, bewildered. But Bram was being pulled along by the line, which had begun heading inside. His face looked blank and unwelcoming.

"Ooooh, the older guy!" Robert began making squeaky kissing sounds.

Sammie rushed at Robert, trying to punch him. He dodged. Her fist flung out and hit air.

"You punch like a girl," taunted Robert.

The bunched line of Bram's classmates was being swallowed by the school's double doors. Helplessly, Sammie watched as Bram stepped inside. He hadn't said one word to stick up for her against the two bullies. Robert and Mark danced out of reach into the playground.

She was left red-faced and miserable on the asphalt, opening and closing her hands. She hated boys. Hated them. All of them—even Bram.

After school, she trudged home from the bus stop feeling dismal. She wouldn't go to Winghaven today, she decided. She couldn't stop thinking about the expression on Bram's face. He looked like he hated her.

She knew Bram wouldn't ask Vicky if she could stay with them now. And since she'd broken their pact, maybe he'd feel free to bring any new friends he wanted to Winghaven.

She was sitting listlessly at the kitchen table when her mother got home.

"Is everything okay?" asked her mom, surprised. Sammie wasn't one to sit still for long. Besides, normally when her parents arrived, Sammie was upstairs carefully hiding away her day's finds in her Science Room.

"I hate school," said Sammie.

Her mom gave her a look of sympathy and worry. She sat down next to Sammie. "Have those boys in your class been bothering you again?"

"You know about that?"

"I had a conversation with your teacher the other day. She let me know you've been having trouble. Next time, you tell me, okay? Don't hide it."

Her mom's sympathy made Sammie's words come out in a rush. "Robert and Mark teased me about Bram being my boyfriend and he is *not*," she said. "And plus, I . . . I broke a promise to Bram, and now he's mad at me."

Her mom slipped her arm around Sammie. "I'll talk to Mrs. Gladwell again." She looked down at Sammie with concern. "Is there anything I can do to help with Bram?"

"I don't think so," said Sammie miserably. But her mom's arm felt reassuring around her. She leaned her head against her side.

"Bram's a nice kid," said her mom. "Do you think maybe you could go over and apologize? Maybe he's not as mad as you think."

Sammie sighed. "Maybe," she said. It felt better to be safe at home, away from everyone who hated her, with her mom's attention on her. "Robert's always so mean."

"School's almost over for the summer, sweetheart," said her mom. She gave Sammie a squeeze. Then her face brightened. "Besides, camp starts in a week, remember?"

The words struck Sammie like a blow.

"Mom, I just can't go to that camp!" she exclaimed. "Robert's going to be there!"

"I can ask them to put you in a different group than Robert, Sammie. You won't have to spend time with him."

She could hear the hurt surprise in her mom's voice— that the very thing she'd thought up to help Sammie was so unwelcome. But her mom mentioning camp—today of all days, the very day she'd lost her chance to spend the summer with Bram—felt like the last straw. Sammie's voice trembled as it rose.

"I just can't go. I *won't* go. You can't make me!"

"Sammie, don't shout. We've been through this already. You're all signed up. We've even paid the deposit."

The tightening tone of her mom's voice was a warning. But Sammie didn't care.

"I'm old enough to stay home by myself!" she yelled as loud as she could. "I'm eleven! If *you* were ever around, you'd understand me!"

She pushed off her mom's arm and ran upstairs, ignoring her mother, who shouted after her: "Samantha! I don't care how upset you are—you don't yell at me!"

Sammie flung herself on the bed and covered her head with a pillow. She felt like her chest would explode.

Her mother's stony expression the next morning told Sammie all she needed to know. Camp was a done deal. Sammie decided not to go to Winghaven that day, either. She didn't want to face Bram. The blank face he'd turned on her, as if he didn't even want to acknowledge she was alive, was stuck in her head.

If he cared about her friendship, he would've defended

her yesterday. He wouldn't have let Robert and Mark be mean to her like that.

If he wanted to stay friends, she thought, he'd come find her himself.

But he didn't. Not at school, not at home.

The next day Sammie woke up with a sense of dread. Camp was days away now. If she didn't go to Winghaven this week, she wouldn't see it again for months. She would go there today and find Bram, and if he didn't say anything mean, *maybe* she'd apologize. *Maybe.* If he didn't want to be friends anymore, she thought, picking up her chin defiantly, she would just bird-watch in a different part of Winghaven on her own. Things would be like they used to be. Winghaven was a big place—it would have to be large enough for both of them.

She biked there fast but walked down the entry path extra slowly. Breaking through the trees, she turned her eyes to Bram's boulder.

But he wasn't there.

She wandered around awhile, looking for him, but he was nowhere to be found. She thought she would be relieved, but instead her heart sank into her shoes.

He'd given up not just on her but on Winghaven itself.

17

THE PROJECT

On Saturday, Sammie biked determinedly to Winghaven. She would at least enjoy her usual time here to herself. But the day felt flat, the grasses quiet. She saw a rabbit and a few birds, but nothing gave her the usual thrill.

The next day, her feet pedaled her past the entrance to Winghaven.

She would go to Bram's and say sorry, like her mom suggested. If Bram hated her now—well, anything was better than not knowing either way.

She let her bike down on Bram's driveway. Taking a deep breath, she marched up to the front door. Then she knocked.

Vicky opened the door. Her eyebrows lifted. "Oh!" she said. "Sammie. I didn't think it would be you. Bram's not here."

In the silence after Vicky's words, Sammie could hear her heartbeat roaring in her ears. Even Vicky knew about their argument.

"Okay," she said, voice muffled. She turned hastily away and began hurrying back down the walkway.

I won't cry, she told herself fiercely, dribbles of water leaking from her eyes. *I won't.*

"Sammie?" Vicky called. Sammie kept her head down— she didn't want Vicky to see her tears. Vicky's voice sounded again. "You didn't find Bram at that old lot you two play in?"

Sammie stopped short.

In a rush she realized how much she wanted to share Winghaven with Bram. She knew now that she'd long ago stopped wanting Winghaven for herself. She wanted to arrive to find him there on his boulder, waiting for her before he got up to explore. She missed him. She even missed his brainy, know-it-all ideas.

"Thanks, Vicky. I'll check there!" she called breathlessly over her shoulder. Then she almost flew to her bicycle on the driveway. "If Bram gets back, tell him I'm looking for him!" Her feet were already churning, the summer wind whipping leftover tears from her cheeks.

Leaving her bike, she slipped into the entry path. As she neared the mouth to the grasslands, the day's glow beckoned through the archway of trees. The air smelled warm, like baked bread.

She stepped from the trees into the full brightness of the day. She shaded her eyes.

"Hey."

Bram was sitting on the granite boulder, just as he always had. They stared at each other. Sammie swallowed. Suddenly she didn't know what to say.

"I can leave, if you want," said Bram.

"No," said Sammie quickly. "No, don't leave."

"I thought you must have decided you didn't want to come here anymore," said Bram.

"I did come. But you weren't here," said Sammie.

"I didn't come because you didn't. I thought you were mad at me."

"And I thought *you* were mad at *me*!"

"Well, I was mad," Bram admitted.

Was mad. That sounded like he wasn't mad anymore. Sammie's words came out in a rush. "Are you going to stop being friends with me because of Robert and Mark?"

"What?" Bram looked bemused. "Of course not!"

"They . . . they said the most awful things. And you didn't even stop them."

"You shouldn't listen so much to those stupid kids," said Bram. "They want you to get upset. When you get mad, it's exactly what they want."

"I guess so." Sammie scuffed one foot against the packed dirt.

"I didn't say anything so I wouldn't egg them on."

Again there was a silence. Sammie couldn't look Bram in the eye.

"Anyway, I wasn't mad because of them," he added quietly.

"I know." Sammie dug into herself for the courage to apologize. It was now or never.

"Look, Bram . . . I'm . . . I'm sorry. I'm sorry I didn't tell you about Pete. And that I broke our pact. I won't do it again."

Bram looked over the landscape through his round tortoiseshell glasses. They reflected the light, hiding his eyes, but he still looked sad. He took a deep breath.

"Winghaven is important to me, too," he said.

"Yeah," said Sammie. "I know. Most of all"—she bit her lip and admitted what was hardest for her—"I'm sorry I said Winghaven was *my* place. I . . . I really hated it when you weren't around."

There was a long silence. At last Bram spoke again. "Same here," he said. "I actually came to apologize, too. I thought I might've messed everything up."

"Nuh-uh." Sammie offered a cautious smile. "It was my fault for getting mad at you."

Bram sat quietly for a moment. Then he picked up a pine cone and threw it at her playfully.

"You're dumb," he said. "How come you make such a big deal out of everything, huh?"

Sammie's whole body filled with relief. She grinned.

Bram sprang up from the boulder. "Now we have to make up for lost time!" He punched her shoulder, not too hard. "Come on, let's get started. We still need to think about what project we're going to do together."

"You . . . you're still going to ask your mom about this summer?"

Bram got an impish expression on his face. "I already asked." He shone down a beatific smile. "I just couldn't believe you'd stay mad at me forever."

"And she said yes!" squealed Sammie. She jumped up and down. "This is going to be the best summer ever!"

"Hey, slow down. Your mom's still got to agree, remember?"

"Right." Sammie gazed down the slope at the waving grasses of Winghaven. She just had to believe she would be able to stay here this summer. She'd found the courage to say sorry to Bram—she could find it in her to talk to her mom, too.

Her mind was churning. Bram wanted to do a big project together, and now she was determined to become scientific collaborators, not just friends watching nature together. How could they capture this perfect place? What project would show how the animals and plants of Winghaven depended on and needed one another? She knew they did.

The grasses housed the mice and sparrows, their tall

stalks providing these animals with seeds. Robins nested in the saplings of the hollow. Even the dead trees were important, providing a lookout for predators like the Cooper's hawk she'd once seen alight on the old snag by the path. The bird probably used the tree to gaze out over Winghaven for small mammals he could catch.

But how did all this add up to a scientific study?

As she gazed, she spotted a monarch, huge, almost saucer-size, dancing over the stems of milkweeds tall enough now to be seen among the grasses.

The sight triggered a memory of the article she'd once seen in the paper, of the fragile monarch in the photo, its warning of the threat to monarchs from milkweed loss. Her mind filled with a cascade of images. Pete's marked-off study plots in the woods, his laundry baskets, his notebooks. Insects. Pete studied insects because they were food for birds.

She'd sworn not to talk to Pete again—and this time, she planned to keep her promise. She couldn't risk losing Bram again. But she realized she could maybe still learn something from him.

"I think I have an idea, Bram," she said slowly.

"Oh yeah?"

"I read in the news that monarchs are endangered because there aren't enough places with lots of milkweed," she said. "But Winghaven has tons of milkweed and plenty of monarchs, too. We could look for monarch caterpillars on the milkweed plants and count how many there are."

"Huh," said Bram. "That's neat."

"And it really would show how everything in Winghaven is connected," Sammie said. "The monarchs need milkweed to lay their eggs. But the milkweed needs things from Winghaven, too. It needs other insects and birds to pollinate its flowers. It needs deer and rabbits to eat away shrubs and help keep this a meadow. It even needs the weather. Like the rain and the breeze to blow its seeds around to make more milkweed plants."

"And the deer and the bugs and the birds need Winghaven, too, because it feeds them and gives them shelter!" said Bram.

"Exactly," said Sammie. "They're here because of Winghaven, and Winghaven is here because of them."

"That's perfect, Sammie," said Bram. "Perfect."

He didn't need to say more. They stood shoulder to shoulder in a silence of total understanding, watching the monarch under the warm June sun, basking in the beauty of their idea.

"So when should we start?" said Bram, grinning suddenly, with a little leap like a happy fawn.

Sammie set her chin. "Not yet," she said firmly. "First I'm going to talk to my mom."

18

A SIXTH SENSE
FOR BIRDS

A little reluctant to leave the inviting expanses of Winghaven, they slowly stepped into the dimness of the tree-lined entry path. But almost immediately they stopped short.

In the middle of the path stood a long leggy figure.

"It's Pete!" whispered Sammie in a choked voice. What should she do now?

Pete was leaning forward, peering into the woods through binoculars like someone squinting through a microscope. Standing, he was exceedingly tall and scraggly. His crutches were gone.

He took a few rapid steps, crouched, and brought his binoculars back to his eyes. Then he became aware of Sammie and Bram and looked up.

He lifted his fingers to his lips in a silent *shhhh*.

Their naturalists' instincts took over. They froze, trying to see what Pete had spotted without moving a muscle.

Pete crooked his finger, beckoning.

They crept closer. But only a thicket of brush met their gaze.

Pete murmured so quietly they could barely hear him. "Look at that hump of leaves and mud. To the left of the tuft of reddish leaves."

Pete's instructions made sense of the disorganized forest floor. Sammie now spotted a small mound clearly different from the ground around it. She brought up her binoculars.

It was shaped like a little hut, rounded and thatched of meshed grasses and leaves. In front, it had a round hole.

"Watch."

It didn't take long. A little face appeared at the hole. A face with a beak and a bright eye circled by a white eye ring. Black speckles adorned the bird's white breast. It ran forward on little pink legs. Then it took off and flew furtively into the underbrush. Bram's camera clicked and clicked.

"An ovenbird," said Pete in a normal voice, once the little bird was gone.

"The ones with a really loud call!" exclaimed Sammie.

"That's right! They sing *pitchoo, pitchoo, pitchoo* all summer. They're not easy to see. And the nests are even harder to spot. But I saw that little lady creeping about on the forest floor like she didn't want to be noticed. I knew she might lead me to her nest." Pete chuckled in a pleased way. "You can see why they're called ovenbirds now, hm?"

"The nest looks like a little pizza oven," said Sammie.

Bram had a sullen expression on his face. Sammie flicked him a worried look. Silently she willed him to understand that Pete was one of them. Couldn't he see it?

"Pete, this is Bram," she said. "I didn't get to introduce him the other day."

Pete turned and smiled. "Aha. You're the photographer."

Bram couldn't resist claiming the title. "That's me," he said.

"That's an impressive-looking instrument," said Pete.

Bram clutched his camera closer. "Yeah, it's top of the line," he said.

"I've been thinking of buying a decent camera myself," said Pete. "I liked photography when I was younger."

Bram shrugged and looked away.

"But I don't know what to buy," Pete added, smiling thoughtfully. "Would you mind if I look at yours?"

Pride won out. Slowly Bram held out his precious camera.

Pete accepted it with hands that seemed too big, his knuckles knobbed, palms broad. Yet they cradled the camera like a baby animal.

Slowly he browsed back through Bram's pictures. "You do beautiful work with it," he said. "These ovenbird shots are downright professional, even though I caught you by surprise."

Bram tried to look modest, but Sammie could see his satisfaction.

"This place," said Bram, "it's Sammie's and mine. We know everything about it. We've been working here all spring."

Pete nodded gravely. "Good news to have a couple of wood sprites like you watching over it."

Sammie liked that. A wood sprite. But Bram's black brows drew together. "We're naturalists, not sprites."

Sammie jumped in before Bram could say more.

"It's getting late," she said. "We'd better go."

Pete inspected his watch. "I'd better be along, too. I'll walk out with you two. I drove here today."

Their feet crunched quietly on the path. No one spoke. The silence made Sammie uncomfortable. But when she glanced up at Pete, he had such a placid expression on his long, patient face, a smile playing around his mouth, that she felt reassured.

Reaching the entrance, they turned to him. His car, a battered red station wagon stuffed with equipment, was parked on the roadside in a gravel pullout.

"Are you going to come back?" blurted Sammie, even though she knew she shouldn't.

"Oh, sure," said Pete. "My schedule is flexible ever since I graduated."

He was facing away from Winghaven, looking toward them as he talked. Behind him stood the line of tall mixed oaks and pines. He paused. Then, in one fluid motion, he twisted around and lifted his arm, pointing into the air behind him. "Look," he said. "A turkey vulture."

At the very moment that he said it, they saw it. The huge, dark, kitelike shape of a turkey vulture lifted over the tree-tops. It teetered there, perfectly in view. Then it rose on a draft of warm air and swung off sideways, disappearing once again behind the tree line.

Sammie and Bram stared at Pete in wonder.

He simply smiled. "Have a good afternoon, you two." Then he opened his car door and swung his beanpole legs into the front seat. He started the beat-up old station wagon and slowly rolled away.

Sammie and Bram were left open-mouthed on the road.

"How did he know that was there?" exclaimed Bram. "It was behind him!"

"Maybe he heard it?"

"A turkey vulture? They don't call, and their wings don't

make any noise. He must have seen its shadow on the road."

"He spotted it before we did! And we were looking right at the trees."

Bram shook his head wonderingly. "That's amazing," he said. "He must have a sixth sense for birds."

Sammie said nothing. Maybe, just maybe, Bram would come around to liking Pete after all.

WEATHER: Hot, sunny, dry
LOCATION: Entry path, Winghaven
TIME: 4:45 p.m.

OVENBIRD!
(found by Pete)

Her nest is thatched
out of sticks.
So well camouflaged
it's hard to see!

black — orange crown

white eye ring

light
brown

heavily streaked/
speckled with black
on white breast

pinkish

long fingerlike feathers

holds wings in "V"
shape

Turkey vulture over
the pines—just before
heading home

19

COURAGE

It was time to take the plunge.

Sammie's mom was humming to the radio, stirring dinner on the stove, and drinking a glass of her favorite wine. Sammie's dad had brought her mom flowers as an end-of-the-weekend treat. She was relaxed, acting like her old self for once.

Sammie fixed the image of the monarch in her mind and of Bram's face as he'd said, *That's perfect. Perfect.*

"Mom, can I talk to you?"

"Of course, sweetheart." Her mom's face shifted to concern. "What's the matter?" She sat down at a kitchen chair.

Sammie steeled herself and opened her mouth. Then she closed it again. Then she opened it. She couldn't lose Winghaven now.

"I don't want to go to camp this summer."

Her mother's expression fell. "Oh, Sammie, this again?"

"No, please, Mom, listen to me." Sammie spoke fast,

clinging to her determination. "I told you the boys who hate me will be at Camp Shriver. And I don't fit in with the kids from my school." She hadn't planned to cry, but she felt tears prickling the corners of her eyes.

"I went and apologized to Bram like you told me to, and we made up. Then he invited me to spend the days at his place this summer instead."

If she was going to tell her mom about Winghaven, now was the time.

She hesitated. She hadn't exactly *lied*. More just . . . left out a bit of the truth. What if it made her mom say no?

"I . . . I wouldn't be on my own, then" was all she said. "It would fix everything."

"Sammie, sweetheart." Her mom reached out and gently patted her hand. "Let's be realistic. We can't ask his mom to watch you all summer. It's too much responsibility."

"Vicky already said yes. She's home painting all day anyway, she said."

"She did?" Her mom inspected her. "Bram asked her? It wasn't you who asked?"

"No, Mom, I wouldn't, I swear."

Her mom looked into Sammie's hopeful face. "I do like Bram," she said. "He's a nice, responsible boy."

Sammie held her breath and gazed at her mom with tear-filled eyes.

Her mom rubbed her forehead. "We've already paid the deposit," she said. "But they might still give us a refund. And I guess it would save money in the long run. Let me give Vicky a call. Meanwhile, you go upstairs and ask your dad."

The tight bands clenched around Sammie's heart sprang free. Whenever her mom told her to ask her dad, Sammie knew she had won.

"Oh, thank you, thank you, thank you!"

Her mother gave a rueful laugh. "Now, now, your dad hasn't said yes yet. Go on upstairs."

Sammie trotted up to her dad's office. He rolled back his chair from his computer.

"What is it, honey?" He peered at her through his black-rimmed glasses. "Have you been crying? Come sit by me." He patted the chair beside him.

Sammie sat down and leaned her head against him while he wrapped an arm securely around her. Her dad might live in his own head, but he always made her feel accepted. She told him about Robert at school. She told him about how she and Bram watched nature together, leaving out Winghaven but telling him about Bram's camera and the birds they saw on the neighborhood streets, and how Vicky was always home painting.

"I don't want to go to camp, Dad. I want to keep learning

things here with Bram," Sammie said passionately, sitting back and looking at him. "Can I stay at his place instead?"

Her dad rocked thoughtfully back and forth in his office chair. "Well, now," he said. "What does your mother say?"

"She said she'll talk to Vicky," Sammie said. "And told me to ask you. Please, Dad?"

"I don't see why not," said her dad. "Not if you're over at Bram's."

Sammie jumped up. She put her arms around her dad's neck and gave him a kiss. "Thanks, Daddy," she said.

"My little explorer," said her dad. "I'm glad you've found a friend who likes nature as much as you do."

Sammie pounded back downstairs. She could hear her mom talking on the phone with Vicky. She burst back into the kitchen, only to stop short.

Her mom's face was grim. She hung up the phone.

"Vicky said you and Bram have been going to that big abandoned lot together," said her mother, voice tense.

Sammie's whole body tightened up.

Oh *no*.

"I told you never to go down there, Sammie."

Sammie found it difficult to speak past the scared lump in her throat.

"But—but I'm not going by myself," she managed. "I'm going with Bram."

"I thought I told you to only go there with me."

"But, Mom, you're always at work!" Sammie burst out. "I'd never get to go!"

"Sammie, I expect you to do what you're told, even if I'm not home." Her mom sighed and frowned. She looked as much distressed as angry. "I've asked Vicky to have you two kids stay out of there."

"Mom!" A sense of injustice rose in Sammie's throat. She needed Winghaven. Suddenly she felt her tongue come unglued. As if Sammie were writing in her journal, the words seemed to flow.

"You think it's just an old empty lot, but it's so much more. It's full of birds and animals and plants, and I learn everything I want to know there. I take my binoculars, and Bram takes his camera, and we try to become real scientists. Look—" With a shaking hand, Sammie pulled her bird book out of her pack. She turned the pages, showing her mom each check mark on the top right corner that she'd scrawled on each bird she'd seen. "I've seen all these birds, and I'm learning how science class at school connects to the plants and creatures that live there. It means everything to me. It's important—*please* don't take it away."

Her mom looked upset and unconvinced. Sammie could see a "no" gathering. She realized her lie might be what ended up tipping her mom's decision. Why hadn't she listened to Bram and just told the truth?

A voice came from behind. "Susan, I think this is really important to Sammie. I think we should let her go."

Sammie almost jumped out of her skin. She'd been so focused on her mom that she hadn't heard her dad come downstairs behind her.

He ambled into the kitchen as she stared at him in shock. He *never* went against her mom's decisions about her. Her mother, too, looked taken aback.

"If they're together, I'm sure Bram will look after Sammie," he said.

Sammie felt a confusing mix of comfort and insult. She could take perfectly good care of herself, thank you very much. But her dad was sticking up for her!

Her mom stared at her dad for a moment. "Samantha, go wait in your room."

Sammie turned and hurried upstairs. But instead of going into her room, she shut her bedroom door to make it sound as if she had. Then she crept back to sit and listen at the top of the stairs.

"They're still so young, Dave. Two kids on their own in a big empty place like that . . ."

"Bram's a big kid now, starting junior high. Why not have

Sammie take a cell phone and call you during the day to let you know how it's going?"

Sammie crossed her fingers, clamped her hands into fists, and squeezed her eyes shut.

Her mom sighed. "Vicky said it would help her a lot for Bram to have company this summer."

"Well, there you go!" Her dad's voice was bright with satisfaction.

"But I don't want to reward Sammie for her behavior, Dave. First, she's been letting her temper get away from her. And worse, she lied to me. How can I trust her?"

The words hurt. Sammie didn't want her mom to think that way about her. *You keep too many secrets,* Bram had said.

"This past year has been a hard time for Sammie. She got uprooted from her old school and house, she's had a tough adjustment to the new school, and we both started working. It's a lot of change."

Her mother gave a reluctant grunt.

"And Sammie . . . she's just different, Sue. She's an unusual kind of kid. She needs space to stretch her wings in her own way."

Their voices got quieter. Sammie strained to hear.

"Samantha!" Her mom's call, loud and firm, startled Sammie.

Sammie walked downstairs as if to her own execution. She stood feeling guilty and scared and very small.

"I don't like this, Sammie. I especially don't like that you've been sneaking there without telling me. It was important to me that I could trust you with the responsibility of being home alone."

Sammie swallowed. She had found it in her to apologize to Bram—she could do the same now.

"I'm sorry I lied to you, Mom," she said. "It was wrong."

Her mother studied her. "That's a start."

Sammie stared at her shoes.

"You don't go there on your own, do you? Only with Bram?"

At that moment Sammie made a decision. No more going to Winghaven alone.

"No, Mom." That was the last lie she'd tell. "And I promise I never will."

Her mother rubbed a hand through her bobbed brown hair. "I know this hasn't been an easy move for you. And both your dad and I can tell how much this place means to you. So if you stick with Bram, and if you call me twice a day, Sammie, you can go."

Sammie reached her arms around her mom's neck and hugged her tight.

20

SURPRISES

"Bram, stop that banging, for heaven's sake."

Vicky's voice was half-garbled by a paintbrush between her teeth as she peered around from her porch studio to where Sammie and Bram had their heads eagerly bent together.

Mostly, Vicky hardly noticed them as she worked. She would wander by unseeingly, fill a cup of tea, and roam back to her painting without speaking. Every so often, though, something cut through her concentration, and she would pop out like a chipmunk from a hole.

Bram quit excitedly thumping his sneaker toe against the kitchen island. "Sorry, Mom," he said.

"You kids," she said tolerantly. She craned her neck to look at the papers scattered in front of them. "Hey, that's a lovely drawing."

"Really?" In front of Sammie lay a large sketch of a monarch butterfly, the beginnings of a logo for their project.

Hearing Vicky, a professional artist, praise her drawing felt good.

Vicky roamed over. "Could I make a suggestion?" she said. "Why don't you—"

"Mom!" Bram interrupted, scowling. "Leave us alone. We're doing it our way."

Vicky smiled and flung up her hands. "Mr. Independent! Okay, okay. I'm going back to my work."

Her long strides took her out to the porch.

"Why'd you say that? Maybe your mom had a good idea."

"Mom wishes I was an artist like her," said Bram. "She wants to get me talking about art. But nature photography is my thing. Besides, I like your sketch as it is."

Sammie couldn't help smiling at that.

A moment later, Bram's dad came roving by and poured a glass of milk. He had sandy-brown hair and a little brown beard and was shorter than Bram's mom, which Sammie found strange. Most days, Bram's dad went in to the university, but some days he stayed at home to work uninterrupted by students and colleagues. With an absent look on his face, he wandered back out of the kitchen, house shoes shuffling against the wood floor.

"Hi, Wesley!" Sammie called out a little mischievously. He reminded her a little of her own dad, and it made her feel comfortable.

"Hm, what?" Bram's dad seemed to emerge from some deep inner well. He turned and blinked at her, then smiled. "Oh, hi there, Samwise." He always called her Samwise after the faithful sidekick in his favorite fantasy novel. Then, clearly still lost in thought, he vanished.

Both Bram's parents seemed to live in a dream world. Sammie could see why Bram said he felt lonely—but then again, it wasn't like he welcomed their input a lot of the time. He seemed just like his parents in some ways, always eager to bury himself in some project that took up his whole attention.

Maybe Sammie was a little bit like that herself, she realized—just like her own dad. Maybe that's why she and Bram got along.

They finished their planning and headed to Winghaven that afternoon to work on their project.

They were going to record each milkweed plant, then count any caterpillars. Sammie was making a painstaking map of the location of each milkweed they found. But on plant after plant, they were coming up empty for caterpillars. And there were so many milkweeds. Sammie wasn't sure she could keep them all straight.

After twenty milkweeds or so, Sammie sat down despondently on the path.

"We're doing something wrong, Bram."

"Maybe Winghaven's milkweed is the wrong kind," he said.

"I don't think that can be it," said Sammie. "I'm sure it's regular common milkweed."

Bram frowned. "Or maybe this part of Winghaven doesn't have that many caterpillars for some reason. Predators or something. Let's check the south half of the Field."

They marched determinedly down the path and around the corner.

Finding Pete was so unexpected, they almost tripped over him.

He was lying flat on the path, gazing upward. His binoculars rested on his chest.

Sammie blinked at him. "What are you doing?"

"I'm watching for gulls," he said. "Sometimes Iceland gulls pass by here. Their wingtips are pale instead of black like the herring gulls."

Sammie and Bram craned their necks to look upward. A few pale shapes of seagulls drifted by overhead on silent, graceful wings.

"More herring gulls," said Pete. "They're headed to the town dump to steal scraps."

Somewhat to Sammie's surprise, it was Bram who spoke.

"Can you tell us about anything else out here?"

Bram was studying Pete through his glasses with an intent look under his bowl of hair, as if to figure him out.

Pete sat up. "Lots," he said. "Do you want me to?"

"*I* do," jumped in Sammie. She gave Bram a hopeful glance.

Bram looked at Pete with a mixture of challenge and curiosity on his pale, dark-browed face.

"Me too," he said.

Pete rubbed his chin thoughtfully. "All right." He hopped to his feet. "Follow me."

21

ANTLiONS

Sammie and Bram trotted after Pete's long-legged stride down the path through Winghaven.

At the gap in the stone wall, just before the woods, Pete turned aside. He crouched by the stacked flat rocks.

The ground was open and sandy. No plants grew here, except for a few lonely tufts of grass that had managed to find a foothold. Sunlight warmed the bright yellow-white sand.

"Look."

Bram and Sammie saw a dozen small, cone-shaped dents, each no wider than a dime. It looked like someone had poked in the point of an ice-cream cone, over and over.

"What are those?" Bram's dark hair quivered as he bent closer.

"Watch."

A few carpenter ants—the big black kind, the size of a

grain of rice—were wandering by. Pete swiftly plucked one between his finger and thumb, careful not to squash it. Then he flicked it into one of the conical pits.

The ant, finding itself on steep walls of sand, began trying to climb. But the grains slipped under its feet. The small black creature slid downward.

"Poor thing." Sammie reached to try to help it from the hole.

Pete put out a hand to stop her.

The ant's slipping footsteps brought it closer, closer to the bottom of the pit. Then, to their shock, the children saw sprays of sand spitting out from the very bottom of the pit. Fling, fling. The sprays made the ant slip still faster, no matter how hard it struggled. As the ant slithered to the very bottom of the cone, a flurry burst from below. A dark shape leaped up. It snatched the ant from the pit. As fast as a closing mouth, sand collapsed to cloak the opening. The whole vision vanished—and the cone in the sand sat still and quiet in the sun, as before.

Sammie clapped her hand to her mouth.

"Wow!" squealed Bram. "What was that?"

"An antlion," said Pete. "Aren't they incredible?"

"Yeah!" exclaimed Bram, wide-eyed. "What are they?"

"Antlions are insects," said Pete. "They're larvae, not adults—in other words, they're babies, like a caterpillar is the larva of a butterfly. As larvae, they have jaws as long as their bodies. They build sand-pit traps like these. If an ant or spider or anything else stumbles into the hole, the antlion eats it. Eventually, the antlion locks itself underground and changes into an adult antlion, a kind of fly with lacy wings. The adults lay their eggs in the sand, and then the cycle starts all over again."

Sammie had said nothing. She felt a little ill. Pete had thrown an ant to the lion. It had been busily living its life, and Pete had cut it short.

"Antlions like sandy places under trees, protected from rain," Pete went on. "That's why they're here."

"That's amazing," said Bram.

They got up and strolled back up the path. No one seemed to notice Sammie's silence. She felt confused. She had liked Pete, but he'd killed an ant before her very eyes. True, he hadn't really killed it—the antlion had done that. But the ant wouldn't have died if it hadn't been for Pete and—worse still—if it hadn't been for her. He'd sacrificed it to show her something.

Bram was still asking Pete questions. Sparrows flitted across their path as they walked.

At the edge of the woods, Pete stopped.

"You're quiet, Sammie," he said. "Is something wrong?"

Sammie didn't want to talk about it. She didn't want to

seem like a baby. But she found herself blurting out all at once, "You killed that ant! It was happy and alive, and you killed it."

"He didn't kill it!" protested Bram. "He fed the antlion with it."

"But it wouldn't have died if it wasn't for us!" Sammie's voice was a little wail. "It's our fault!"

Pete looked at her thoughtfully. Then he said, "Come over here. Let's talk about it."

He strode over to the boulder where Bram usually waited. Seated, he was as tall as Sammie and a little shorter than Bram. Sammie edged up to him.

"Listen. Do you have a dog?"

Pete's question didn't seem to have to do with anything. "No."

"Well, if you did, what would you feed it?"

"Dog food," she said.

"Yes," said Pete. "What's in dog food?"

Sammie's frown deepened. "Meat."

"Right," said Pete mildly. "Dogs are adapted to eating meat. A diet of only vegetables would make your dog sick. But that meat came from an animal."

"But . . ." said Sammie. *That's different,* she wanted to say. But at the moment she couldn't see exactly how.

"We shy away from death, because we don't see it very

much, you know?" Pete went on. "When we feed a dog ground-up meat from a can, we don't have to see the animal die."

"I guess," said Sammie reluctantly.

"I've always believed we should be able to face death," said Pete. "If we spend all our time running away from it, we won't live fully. We'll be closing our eyes to the earth and its cycle of life."

Sammie pondered his words. It was true, what he said. Death was a natural part of the world, the partner of life. And she ate meat herself. Somehow she'd never thought about it too much; she'd taken her food for granted, eating what her mom put on her plate. Perhaps she should become a vegetarian. But plants were alive, too, and she would still have to eat *them.*

Yet . . . something still felt different about what Pete had done. She squinched her eyes shut. Living beings were so beautiful—why should they have to suffer and disappear?

"I don't like things to die if they don't have to." She swallowed past the lump in her throat. "We only killed the ant to see what would happen. For fun. We could've just looked up what antlions do on the internet."

Pete locked his hands together and leaned forward over his knees. "I suppose I hadn't thought of it that way."

"I feel like creatures should live as long as they can."

"That's a brave and compassionate way to feel, Sammie. Don't change that. It's right."

"You really think so?"

"Yeah." Pete smiled. "I won't feed the antlions again, okay? I'll let them catch their own food."

"Really?"

"I promise."

The edge of Sammie's mouth turned up cautiously. Pete smiled back, the corners of his eyes crinkling, transforming his face into the gentle scarecrow she had so liked from the start. Then he smacked his knees lightly with both hands and rose. "Thanks for joining me this afternoon, you two. I'd better be getting along."

Bram had kept quiet so far. But now he smiled. "Thanks for showing us the gulls and the antlions, Pete," he said.

"Sure thing," said Pete. He brushed off his pant legs and strode away, out into the Field. They watched his tall frame grow smaller as he hiked down the path, his binoculars swinging at his side.

"Maybe you were right," said Sammie. "Sometimes it's better to do things our way."

"Maybe," said Bram. "But Pete is amazing. So you were right, too."

WEATHER: Wet, cloudy, just stormed—finally a little cooler
LOCATION: Winghaven—exploring with Pete near The Pond
TIME: 10:00 a.m.

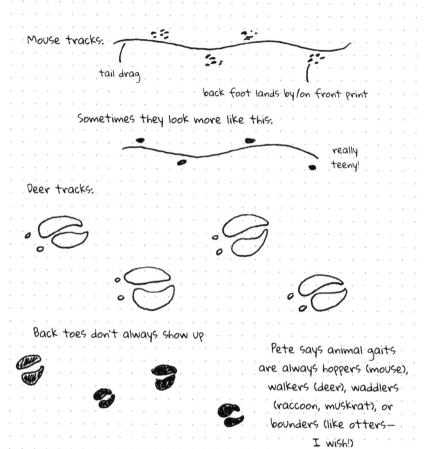

Mouse tracks:

tail drag

back foot lands by/on front print

Sometimes they look more like this:

really teeny!

Deer tracks:

Back toes don't always show up

Pete says animal gaits
are always hoppers (mouse),
walkers (deer), waddlers
(raccoon, muskrat), or
bounders (like otters—
I wish!)

Raccoon tracks:

just like little feet and hands—long toes

22

MILKWEED

Pete began showing up every two or three days. They never quite knew when he might appear. Once, they found him flat on his stomach, peering into a hole. "Vole went in there," he said briefly. They sat down nearby, but he said nothing more, and after what felt like an eternity, they glanced at each other and silently left him there, waiting for the small mouselike animal to come back out.

But usually he looked delighted to see them. He'd explain what he was looking at or drop what he was doing and suggest some new adventure.

With Pete, they spotted their first ruffed grouse and their first woodcock, round as a candlepin bowling ball but motionless—fist-size, dappled, with a huge black eye and a long bill, frozen in place among a net of leaves. They withdrew on soft feet, leaving the little bird alone.

After a rainstorm, Pete appeared like a hare from the wet

woods and led them to the mud surrounding the Pond. He showed them mouse tracks, deer tracks, raccoon tracks. Sammie knew some of these but had never seen coyote tracks before Pete pointed them out.

One afternoon, as they were about to do their regular check under the old door, Bram ruffled the thick leaves of a lanky milkweed plant. He sighed.

"We're not getting anywhere on our project, Sammie."

"I know," said Sammie a little unhappily.

Their frustration at finding no monarch caterpillars had made it easy to let their project fall by the wayside. What with Pete's unexpected appearances and his suggestions for things to look for, they'd been focusing on his ideas instead of their own. They'd checked the milkweeds in the south half of Winghaven, then tried the north half again. But still, no luck. And neither of them wanted to admit their idea wasn't working. Maybe it meant Winghaven was less important than they thought.

Sammie hefted up the door. Just a couple of worms half exposed on the soil. Startled by the rush of air, they contracted their long damp bodies to pull themselves deeper into the earth.

"Maybe we should think up something different."

Sammie slowly set the door down. She didn't want to give up. Winghaven should be perfect for monarchs. The adult butterflies fluttered by all the time. She just had to be right about the milkweed.

She eyed Bram cautiously. Pete studied insects for a living. And he was their friend now, right?

She took a deep breath. "Listen, Bram. Just listen, don't get mad. Why don't we talk to Pete about our project? I bet he'd know what we're missing."

Bram's brows drew together.

"You already said we can't ask my dad. I want this to be ours, yours and mine."

"I know." Sammie took a deep breath. She probably shouldn't have said that. "But just listen. We already came up with our own idea. Pete told me it's important to have scientific collaborators—and now that's what *you* are, you know? My collaborator. More than ever this summer."

Bram didn't look at her but seemed to smile a little at her words.

"Now we're stuck, and we could really learn something from Pete. Just like Jane Goodall did from her scientific adviser."

Bram looked out over the meadow. "Well . . ." he said slowly, "my dad always does say that when scientists share their ideas, they make more progress."

Sammie nodded eagerly. "You see?"

There was a long pause as Bram seemed to wrestle with his thoughts.

"Next time we see Pete," he said, finally, "let's ask."

Two days later, Sammie sat on the hillock with Pete and Bram, intently explaining their monarch project to the scientist: their milkweed maps, their failures.

When Sammie finished, Pete looked at her with an odd expression on his face, a mix of admiration and a kind of puzzled surprise.

"You have an excellent scientific instinct, Sammie," he said. He paused, seeming to think deeply, before adding, "A professional couldn't have come up with a better idea."

"Really?" Sammie filled up with warmth like the grasses in the summer sun.

"Really. The only reason you're not finding caterpillars is because it's too early in the season. For now you'll only find eggs smaller than a pinhead, and maybe some caterpillars the size of a thistle seed."

"Right!" exclaimed Bram. "Why didn't we think of that, Sammie?"

"And I'd only suggest a few changes to your counting procedures. They're well designed."

"Bram came up with those," said Sammie loyally.

"You're really a pair of budding experts." Pete rubbed his chin, considering, and finally added, "Let me show you something."

Sammie and Bram gathered close to peer over his shoulder as he opened a web page on his phone.

It read MONARCH LARVA MONITORING PROJECT.

Brightly colored photographs of butterflies and fields filled the page. The website described a project that scientists were working on. To understand changing monarch populations, they were counting monarchs nationwide—tallying eggs, caterpillars, and adult butterflies—as well as keeping track of milkweed species.

"Oh no!" Sammie exclaimed.

Pete looked at her in surprise. "What's the matter?"

"I thought you said I'd had a great idea. But someone else is already doing it, and so much better than we can!"

Pete smiled at her gently. "Sammie, you're only eleven, and all by yourself you thought up an idea that professional scientists are working on. That's pretty amazing, as far as I'm concerned!"

Sammie's throat felt tight. There would be no point, she thought, in doing the scientists' work all over again.

"Besides, look here. This is the most important part." He clicked a link.

"The scientists can't collect enough data on their own,"

Pete said. "So this project asks people to become what they call *citizen scientists*. Citizen scientists do the same work as the professionals and send the scientists their data. See? This is where to enter findings."

He poked the screen, and the boxes of a sign-up form appeared.

"If you join, your project will be useful to more people than just you," Pete said. "You'll be contributing data real scientists can use. And it can help the monarchs, too."

"Huh," said Bram. "Real science, instead of a kids' project. That's actually pretty cool, Sammie."

When Bram put it that way, she felt guilty for getting upset. "Right," she said resolutely.

"Listen," said Pete. "I want you to go home and read up on the project on the MLMP website. And you're going to need to get some things." He rapped his finger on the top of Sammie's notebook and rattled off several requirements. A meter stick. Wooden stakes. A hammer. A measuring tape. String. Sammie wrote it all down.

"I'd better get a wider sun hat, too," said Bram. "All this hanging out in the sun is giving me a sunburn no matter how much sunscreen I wear."

"I never get sunburns," boasted Sammie. In all Bram's time in Winghaven, he hadn't turned one shade less pale—if he got burned, his skin peeled and not a hint of a tan remained.

Sammie was brown as a hazelnut under her sun-bleached hair. "And I don't get poison ivy like Bram, either."

"Well, at least I've never fallen into the pond!" said Bram, grinning and jabbing a finger at Sammie.

Pete's eyes widened. "Did Sammie fall in the pond?"

"Don't you dare!" said Sammie. She tried to tackle Bram, but he ducked away. She chased him, sparrows startling out of the wet sweet fern to either side and settling in the saplings to watch them as they ran by laughing. When they returned, gasping and grinning, Pete was gone.

"Looks like he's left us to figure out what to do next," Sammie said.

23

PLANS

But Pete turned up again at Winghaven the very next day. He was carrying a large canvas bag. Sammie eyed it curiously, but he set it aside.

"Did you read the MLMP website?" he said. "What did you learn?"

"We sure did," said Bram. "We found out that monarch caterpillars have five different life stages. They're called 'instars.' After each stage, the caterpillars shed their skin so they can grow bigger, just like a snake."

"And there are five kinds of milkweed, and monarchs use all of them," said Sammie.

"Excellent." Pete nodded. "Now, I'd really like to keep helping you two out. Only if you want me to, that is." He lifted a questioning gaze with that long-nosed, droopy-eyed, funny smile of his.

"I do," said Sammie immediately.

To her delight, Bram piped up right away. "Me too," he said.

"I've just got one hesitation," Pete said. "It's probably time for you to let your parents know about me."

Sammie's face fell. "I don't think I can do that. My mom might be upset I talked to a stranger. Especially here."

"Hey, I know!" said Bram. "I'll get my parents to invite Pete to come to tea. He was a graduate student at the university—my mom will like that. She has my dad's students over all the time. Then you can tell your mom he's a friend of my family."

A pang made Sammie hesitate. Bram hadn't wanted to like Pete at first, and now he'd get to have Pete meet his family and see his photographs on his laptop and pay attention to him. She wished she could have Pete over for tea and show him her Science Room.

She forced herself to swallow her envy. It was worth it, she told herself—they'd get to work with Pete, and it would be one less thing she'd have to hide. "Okay," she made herself say.

Bram beamed, looking pleased with himself.

"All right, then, here's what I've been thinking," Pete went on. "Sammie, you remember me telling you about the Audubon Society, where I'll be doing the Christmas Bird Count?"

Sammie nodded. She hadn't forgotten anything Pete had told her.

"Every spring, this region's Audubon Society holds a science symposium. They invite local biologists and naturalists to present their latest findings. Can you see where this is going?"

Sammie held her breath. She could, but it seemed too good to be true.

"If I put in a good word for you both," Pete went on, "and you work extra hard, maybe you can show your project right alongside the professionals."

"That would be awesome!" Sammie burst out. "But—" She caught herself. Bram's friendship was more important to her now than this. "I promised Bram we wouldn't share Winghaven with anyone else. We made an exception for you." She looked at Bram anxiously. "Would you want to do it?"

"Are you kidding?" said Bram. His eyes were shining. "Of course I would!"

The warm feeling that was filling up Sammie seemed to grow and spread and include these two people, her partners in science, in a glow of happiness.

"Fantastic. I switched my Christmas Bird Count region to this part of town, you know. I agree with Sammie. Winghaven is the best birding around."

Sammie and Bram exchanged glances, proud that they'd helped prove to Pete how great Winghaven was.

"The bird count's a long time away, but how about you both join me this year? By then, I should know your families well enough that they'll let me bring you along. And it'll give the regional Audubon director a chance to meet the two of you."

Sammie could hardly believe her good fortune. In two afternoons, her summer had turned from the plans and explorations of two kids into something that could transform her into what she'd dreamed of being—a naturalist and scientist, sharing her findings with other scientists.

Bram bumped his shoulder against hers, both of them speechless with excitement.

"Now," said Pete, "I brought some things for you."

He opened the canvas bag.

From inside, he took out two clipboards. One held a stack of paper printed with information and instructions. "Data sheets from the MLMP for you to write down your findings," said Pete. "They're on weatherproof paper that stays sturdy when it gets wet."

Next he gave Sammie and Bram each a ruler and a hand lens—a tiny magnifying glass that folded up into a metal case. Then he pulled out what he said was a rain gauge. It was a long plastic cup that they could push into the ground and would allow them to record how much rain fell on Winghaven every day.

Finally he reached into the capacious pockets of his vest. He drew out two pens. "These are weatherproof, too," he said. "Even on regular paper, your writing won't smear in the rain."

The two of them fingered the equipment, a little awed. "Thanks, Pete," said Sammie. "This is really nice of you."

Then together they bent over the blank data sheets, and Pete explained what they would need to do.

ECOSYSTEM STUDY PROPOSAL:
MONARCHS OF WINGHAVEN

We propose to count monarch
caterpillars in Winghaven to find out
how important Winghaven is to them.
We'll count adult butterflies, too. There
are 2 to 4 generations every summer.

Egg

The first monarchs arrive in New
England in June. The first caterpillars
hatch in July. So we should be just in
time for the "first generation" of
caterpillars.

MONARCH
CATERPILLARS

Grow in
bunches

Flowers
are small
and whitish
purple

MILKWEED:
broad green leaves
on a thick stem

Loss of Milkweed Lands Monarchs on Endangered List

By FRANK WILSON

No butterfly is more iconic than the
regal monarch. Famed for overwintering
by the tens of millions on just a few sites
in the Mexican wilderness, the butterfly
performs a marathon of migration to
North America each summer.

Generations of schoolchildren have
raised monarch caterpillars to adulthood,
learning from them the natural wonder of
metamorphosis.

Yet this symbol of rebirth has now been

**Beloved butterfly and
symbol, once common,
struggles to survive**

classified as "Endangered" by the
International Union for Conservation of
Nature (IUCN).

"The monarch butterfly is a bellwether
of environmental health," said Aubrey
Swift, an insect ecologist with the
Organization for the Protection of
Pollinators. "Because it travels so far,

it needs healthy landscapes across its
migration path."

Most troubling for the monarch, the use
of herbicides on farm crops has led to a
decline in milkweed, the sole food source

for its caterpillars. Monarch butterfly
populations have fallen 80 percent within
three decades, Swift said.

At least one hundred million acres of
milkweed have disappeared, a victim of the

HABITAT A critical food source for monarchs, milkweed has succumbed to herbicides.

Continued on page 4

24

HARD WORK

The next day, Sammie and Bram stared at the broad stretch of grasses and plants rolling over the sloping ground of Winghaven. It looked bigger than ever. Sammie reviewed Pete's instructions in her mind.

"Well," said Bram, taking a deep breath, "I guess we should get started."

They pulled their socks up over their pants and tucked in their shirts to keep out ticks and poison ivy.

Then they waded through the grasses to set up their Study Plot. At each of the four corners of the grassy Field area of Winghaven, they pounded in a wooden stake. Then, with the measuring tape, they measured exactly how big the plot was. Sammie carefully sketched it into her notebook.

By the time they finished, Sammie was sweating. But their day's work had only just begun.

"It's too difficult to keep track of all of Winghaven's

individual milkweeds," Pete had said. "You'll need a milk-weed density for your Study Plot instead."

Following Pete's instructions, Bram threw a pencil into the air. Then, in the direction the pencil pointed, Bram and Sammie stretched a string from one side of the Study Plot to the other so they wouldn't lose track of which direction to walk.

Along the string, they walked ten steps into the Study Plot. They used the meter stick to measure a square that was one meter long on each side. Inside the square, they had to count all the milkweed plants.

"One," said Sammie. The first square seemed a bit disappointing.

Bram was carrying the clipboard of data sheets. He wrote it down.

They walked another ten steps and measured a new square. This one didn't have any milkweeds at all. They walked another ten, and another, each time measuring a meter square and counting the milkweeds inside. Sammie was relieved to find a fair number of squares with five or six plants inside.

When they reached the opposite edge of their plot, Bram said, "Okay. Now it says we have to pick a different direction and do it again." He tossed the pencil again.

After counting forty-seven squares, Sammie flung herself down on her back on the sandy path.

"This is awful," she groaned. "I'm so *hot*."

Bram bent diligently over the data sheet. "It says that the more squares we count, the more accurate our results will be. The calculation averages the milkweed plants we count in randomly chosen squares. The more squares, the more representative the answer will be of Winghaven's actual milkweed density. It says we can count up to one hundred squares."

"One *hundred*?" Sammie stared at Bram in dismay. "But it says we can count less if we want!"

Bram frowned. "But then our numbers won't be as accurate."

"I don't care," groaned Sammie. "I'm sure they're close enough. Let's take a break and look for birds for the rest of the afternoon."

Bram looked at her in disapproval. "I thought you wanted to be a scientist," he said.

Sammie sat up, stung. "I do want to be a scientist." Sullenly she picked up her notebook again. "I was just kidding."

"Hmph," grunted Bram. Sammie hauled herself to her feet and went back to work.

"Hey, who's that?" said Bram as Sammie was bent over their clipboard.

Sammie looked up. Bram was leaning forward, peering intently toward the pine forest beyond the stone wall.

"I don't see anyone."

"I thought I just saw another kid. They stepped out of the woods and then went back in again."

"Are you sure?"

"Pretty sure." Bram frowned. "I couldn't tell if they saw us or not. They were only there for a second."

Sammie stared toward the forest, her frown mirroring Bram's. Had someone new moved here, just like Bram had a few months before? Or was another kid from her school snooping around?

She shook it off. Whoever it was, they were gone. Hopefully, they wouldn't come back.

And the next day, the best part started.

Larva finding.

Every time Sammie or Bram found a monarch egg or a caterpillar, a shout rang out over Winghaven. "Got one!"

Each day, they tallied how many plants they examined and how many eggs and caterpillars they found. Multiplying by the milkweed density would give an estimate of the number of larvae in the whole Study Plot.

The eggs were teeny, as small as the eye of a needle and the color of egg white. Pete had instructed them to look carefully with the hand lenses he had given them. Droplets of milkweed sap could look like monarch eggs sometimes, he said. But actual monarch eggs had ribbed sides that Sammie and Bram could see through the magnifying glass.

Sammie liked the monarch caterpillars even better. Just as they'd learned, the caterpillars ranged in size, from the first instar, smaller than a grain of rice, with tiny feelers that couldn't be seen, to the fifth, as big as Sammie's palm, with long black feelers that reached far over the caterpillar's head.

They were beautiful. They were striped all the way down their bodies with bright yellow and black and white. They looked like the candy rolls that filled Sammie's pillowcase each Halloween.

Bram and Sammie kept track of it all. As summer rolled along, their data sheets filled with numbers. Sammie made sketches of each instar and the eggs. She forgot about the heat in the pleasure and expectation of finding more caterpillars on the next plant.

And every so often, an adult monarch danced over the field in its orange-and-black skirts, a breath of fresh air over their hard work.

DATASHEET #1A: MONARCH DENSITY (WEEKLY SUMMARY)

Use this information to fill in Datasheet #1B Season Summary of Monarch Density.

Date: 8/6   Observers: Samantha Tabitha Smith & Bram Layton   Site Name: Winghaven

Start Time: 3:30 p.m.   Stop Time: 4:30 p.m.   Temp in Shade: 87°F

by Sammie, age 11

Eggs	1st Instars	2nd Instars	3rd Instars	4th Instars	5th Instars	# of Adults (F = female M = male U = unknown)	# Dead (egg or larval stage)	# of Milkweed Plants Observed (use tick marks to represent 1, 5, 10, or 20 plants and record total at end of session)
ℍℍ ℍℍ ℍℍ ℍℍ ℍℍ ℍℍ 11	ℍℍ ℍℍ ℍℍ ℍℍ ℍℍ ℍℍ ℍℍ ℍℍ	ℍℍ ℍℍ ℍℍ ℍℍ ℍℍ 111	ℍℍ 1	111	1	1 F 1 U		ℍℍ ℍℍ ℍℍ ℍℍ ℍℍ ℍℍ ℍℍ ℍℍ ℍℍ 111

Plants in bloom at site (species, not numbers of plants!):

Common milkweed, Queen Anne's Lace, Red Clover, Dandelion, Black-eyed Susan
Joe-Pye Weed, Daisy Fleabane, Goldenrod, Ironweed

Note any disturbances that occurred at the site over the past week (mowing, herbicide spraying, haying, etc.):

Did you see any *Aphis nerii* at your site this week? Circle one: Yes   (No)   Didn't look

Other Notes:

25

CHANGES

As July rolled into August, Pete turned up less often. He said he had a lot of work to do applying for jobs. Mostly, though, he seemed to want to let them manage their study on their own.

Whenever they asked him how to do something or what they should do next, Pete almost never answered directly.

"What do you think?" became his favorite reply.

Even on days when Sammie felt most unsure, Pete's question felt like trust.

The closer the school year came, though, the more distracted Bram seemed. He'd always had his head in the clouds, but recently he'd gotten even more quiet and reserved than usual. He'd even skipped some of their usual Sunday meetups. Bram said he had extra violin practice so he'd be sure to get into the junior high orchestra. Plus, he'd been assigned some books in preparation for the school year. Sammie didn't think any of that was enough reason to seem so out of sorts. Bram was sure to get into the orchestra. And he could read as fast as anyone she knew.

Sammie even mentioned Bram's behavior to her mom one afternoon as they were driving to the mall to buy Sammie new school clothes.

"Bram's probably just adjusting to the idea of a new school, Sammie," said her mom. "The moment he got used to elementary school here, the school year was practically over. Now he's facing another big change. Give him a little space."

As their car passed Sammie's school, her mom slowed down behind the big yellow rear of a school bus.

"That's funny," said her mom. "Oh, it must be the Camp Shriver kids getting home for the day. That could've been you, Sammie. I still think it's a pity you didn't go."

Sammie didn't think it was a pity at all. Instead of camp, she'd spent a glorious summer with Bram and Pete. She just hoped Bram would want to keep working as hard on their project now that he'd be at a whole new school, with new friends and adventures on the horizon.

A couple of kids jumped out of the bus. She spotted an unmistakable shock of black hair and stocky shoulders.

Robert.

Of course. Sammie knew he lived on one of the streets just behind their school, close enough that he walked instead of taking the bus. His neighborhood bordered the western woodland abutting Winghaven.

Robert trotted back along the road straight toward them. He glanced into the car window and looked Sammie right in the eye.

Sammie hastily looked away. It was too late, though. She knew he'd seen her.

The bus rumbled on, and her mom pulled forward. Cautiously, Sammie peered into the car's side mirror.

Robert had reached the intersection with the closest cross street, but he hadn't turned to walk home. Instead, he was staring after their car.

She hoped he wouldn't bug her about what she'd been up to all summer long when she had to see him again.

For the first time in ages, she was thinking about school again, and she didn't like it.

26

THE EGG

When school inevitably began again, Sammie had to admit it was exciting being one of the big kids.

She carefully set up her assigned locker, filling it with her new school supplies but also with a spray of dried grasses and flowers from Winghaven and a couple of extra field guides in case she spotted anything interesting during recess.

Robert wasn't in her homeroom this year. Maybe her mom and Mrs. Gladwell had had something to do with it. Sammie felt like she could breathe easier.

She wondered what Pete would get up to now that she and Bram weren't at Winghaven every day. Would he miss them?

The thought brought up other uncomfortable feelings. Today she wouldn't see Bram at recess, not even the brief hellos they used to share. And today he couldn't come to Winghaven because of an after-school meeting.

After a whole summer together, maybe he was tired of spending so much time with Sammie. The bell rang for the start of class, and she pushed the idea away.

"Hey, I have an idea, Sammie." Bram's ideas always seemed to come when Sammie's mind wandered. She brought her attention back to the hot oven of late summer.

She'd been thinking about Pete visiting Bram's house for tea. "My parents loved him," Bram had enthused. "He said he graduated just before the summer, and now he's got a temporary job at the university as a field technician while he looks for something permanent."

Sammie had eyed Bram regretfully. "Was it fun having Pete over?"

"Oh yeah," Bram had said, his eyes far off. "He's so cool. He wanted to see my orienteering maps and hear me play violin and everything."

Sammie looked off over Winghaven's grasses and brush. Only insects broke the heat's dead weight: a loud, rising whine of cicadas, buzzing like a broken machine.

Soon the monarchs would fly away for their long migration. She and Bram had already begun to notice fewer and fewer caterpillars on the milkweed leaves every day. They'd learned that peak migration time for New England was around September 3 to 15. In a few weeks, the monarchs would be mostly gone. And there'd be less reason to go to Winghaven.

Right now, though, she was glad to have Bram come up with a new idea. It felt like he was being his usual self again.

"Let's bring a monarch egg home to my place. We can raise it into a butterfly."

Sammie squinched her mouth up and her eyebrows down. "We'd be taking it from its habitat," she said after a moment.

"But not forever!" said Bram. "Just until it grows up. It'd be safer at my house than in the wild. No predators, and we can feed it milkweed leaves every day."

Would it break Sammie's rule—never to collect anything alive—to take a caterpillar home? She and Bram had already brought pond water home to look at invertebrates. Still, they'd returned the water to nature the very next day.

They'd bring this monarch back to Winghaven eventually, too.

"I read online about how to keep caterpillars," said Bram. "I can show you. And we can report our results to the MLMP. They keep track of how many eggs and caterpillars turn into adults when they're reared away from predators."

They decided the day was too hot for more counting, so they headed back to Bram's to do a little research on his laptop.

Most monarchs live only two to six weeks, they read.

However, four generations of monarchs hatch each summer. The fourth generation almost miraculously lives eight months, long enough to fly to Mexico. But rather than a miracle, it was natural science—the butterflies had adapted over thousands of years so they wouldn't have to survive through freezing northern winters.

"In the north of the US, the last generation of monarchs hatches in August and September," said Sammie.

"That means if we get an egg now, our butterfly could journey all the way to Mexico!" Bram exclaimed.

Back at Winghaven, they chose a fat little egg with care. Gently they plucked its milkweed stem and brought it back to Bram's in a plastic container with holes punched in the top, hoping they had picked one that would successfully hatch.

And it did—but for a couple days, the caterpillar itself was so small that Bram and Sammie couldn't find it, afraid to accidentally squash it if they opened its enclosure to search. When they finally saw it for the first time, lazily munching a milkweed leaf, relief coursed through Sammie's insides like water returning to a dried-up forest creek after a rainstorm.

They housed the caterpillar in Bram's backyard in a wooden and mesh butterfly-raising cage his dad helped them build. They kept it outside, because they'd read that monarchs raised indoors might not learn the natural cues they needed to migrate. Every day they gave it fresh milkweed leaves. A moistened paper towel kept the habitat from drying out. At last, the caterpillar crawled to the top of the cage and hung itself from the wood on a tiny stalk of silk. There, it transformed into a bright green chrysalis. A couple of weeks later, the pupa slowly changed color from green to black.

Bram promised that if the monarch began to emerge when Sammie wasn't around, he'd call her right away.

27

ROBERT

"I can't come out today, Sammie. My mom's taking me into the city to go shopping."

Sammie was at Bram's door. He'd texted her to let her know he couldn't make it to Winghaven, but she'd only gotten his message when she'd arrived at the entry path. So she'd stopped by.

She studied him sorrowfully. "Shopping? What for?"

"Just some new clothes." He looked uncomfortable.

"In the city? Can't you just get them at the mall?"

"Uh." Bram hesitated. "My mom thinks I need some nicer things. Like a suit."

"A suit?" said Sammie, a little horrified. She couldn't imagine him stuffed into a designer suit. Bram belonged in torn jeans and a T-shirt.

"Yeah, for violin and stuff. Auditions or whatever.

Anyway," he spoke hurriedly, and looked back into his house, "I have to go, okay?"

"When are we going to work on our project next, Bram?" asked Sammie. "You've got orchestra tomorrow, and we don't have that long to collect the last of our data."

"I promise I'll be around later this week," he said.

Sammie stood forlornly on the step while he shut the door.

She pedaled slowly back up the street. Auditions. What had that been about? Hadn't he already finished with auditions this fall? For both the school orchestra and the conservatory in the city?

She paused at the opening to Winghaven's entry path, gazing wistfully between the twigs.

She had promised her mother not to go in alone.

It wouldn't do any harm to go in just once, she told herself. These days, it didn't take long to count caterpillars—they were big and easy to find. They were poisonous to most animals and birds from the toxic milkweed sap they consumed, so they didn't have to be hidden to survive. And there weren't as many of them this late in the season. Most had turned into butterflies by now. She could grab the data and get home.

She looked around carefully. Then she slipped in among the branches.

The path opened in front of her, fragrant and familiar,

a scent of soil rising to her nostrils as her shoes squelch-crunched on damp oak leaves. A sense of well-being filled her up as she walked on. Winghaven. Her haven.

She worked her way through their Study Plot, focused on each milkweed plant—the slight fuzziness of the leaves, the way they curled under slightly, hiding the long fat stripy caterpillars. The caterpillars were so big that when the light shone just so, sometimes she could even spot their dark silhouettes through the leaves. Soon she was done. Over the course of the summer, she'd built her ability to work with patience, and now she could work quickly and without distraction.

While she was here, it surely wouldn't hurt to explore a little. She roamed down into the Field. Her old sense of independence and freedom and excitement of adventure welled up inside her as she walked deeper into this landscape that she knew so intimately and yet could always surprise her.

She turned the corner at the Dead Tree, alert to passing birds.

Then, as if in mirror to the day she'd met Bram, she looked down toward the end of the path at the stone wall.

A figure was standing there watching her—the person she least wanted to see.

"Sammie!" Robert shouted.

His voice ringing over Winghaven's serenity made her flinch. Maybe *he* was the kid Bram had glimpsed weeks ago. How dare he come here and frighten all the creatures she and Bram were so careful to keep calm and unfazed by their quiet, unthreatening presence? Anger rushed into her. There was no avoiding Robert now. She had to let him know in no uncertain terms that he wasn't welcome here. That he'd better never come back again.

She marched down the path toward him.

"What are you doing here?" she snapped. "Get out. Now."

"Whoa, cool it, tiger," said Robert. "Jeez. You'd think you owned the place."

"What are you doing here?" Sammie demanded again.

"I live over that way," said Robert. He gestured up the forested slope toward the west, toward Sammie's school and the little neighborhood where she knew he lived.

"That's far away," she said. "There's no reason for you to come out this way."

"I figured you had to be coming here," he said. "I thought I'd check it out."

Sammie flushed. "What do you mean, you figured?"

"You weren't around all summer at Camp Shriver," he said. "And whenever you get a minute at school, you're working on that weird project of yours. I saw you in art class. Plus, I saw a map of this place on your computer one time."

Sammie stared at him open-mouthed. "Why can't you just leave me alone?"

Robert ignored her question. "Walking all the way here down Split Road really sucked."

How could she scare Robert away? Sammie had a brainstorm.

"You better not come here again. Hunters come here, and you might get shot," she lied. "This is my last time for the season."

"That's not true," scoffed Robert. "You can't hunt down here." He pointed toward the Junkyard House. "You're not allowed to hunt closer than three hundred feet to houses. I know 'cause my dad hunts in the woods up behind our place sometimes."

The color drained from Sammie's face. "Your dad hunts in Winghaven?" She was so shocked, she forgot entirely about keeping Winghaven's name to herself.

"Only sometimes. Usually we go up to Maine to hunt."

"*You* know how to hunt? With a *gun*?"

"Yeah, sure. My dad says I'm a good shot." He glanced away over the hills. "It's pretty much the only thing he thinks I *am* good at," he muttered under his breath.

Sammie hardly heard him. Robert was worse than she'd ever dreamed.

"How dare he come here and kill animals?" she said, her

voice a little screech. "This is their home! Where else can they go where they can be safe?"

"Hey, chill out!" said Robert. "They're just animals. They eat each other all the time. What's the difference?"

"It is different!" Sammie had become a towering pillar of anger. "People like you ruin nature for everyone else! You don't need to kill animals—you just do it for fun!"

"How would you know what we need, Snob Girl?" sneered Robert. "Who wants your stupid Winghaven, anyway? My dad says empty land like this is bound to get ripped up for condos."

Sammie went white. She stared at Robert with cold, concentrated fury.

"I hate you," she pronounced, her voice diamond brittle as ice-crusted snow. "Nobody likes you. They pretend to like you because you scare them." Casting for a home for her rage, she snapped out, "I bet your dad doesn't even like you."

Even as she spoke, Sammie realized she'd gone too far.

Robert stared, his face slightly contorted. For a moment, Sammie feared he might hit her. Then to her utter shock, he turned around and ran away, feet thumping heavily on the soil. The sound receded between the pines.

"I didn't mean to say that about your dad!" she shouted.

But she was met by silence.

Sammie trudged slowly back up the path toward home.

At least Robert would probably never come here again, she thought. He was an animal killer and a bully. But why did she feel this aching sense that she was terribly in the wrong?

She stuffed her notebook into her pack, climbed onto her bicycle, and biked home with her head down.

28

LAUNCHING

Sitting on the plastic-covered seat of the bus on the way home from school, Sammie brooded out the window. The bus rattled and bumped, cocooning her in sound.

She hadn't told anyone about running into Robert at Winghaven. Not even Bram. She felt ashamed, both for breaking her promise to her mom and for what she'd said to Robert. At school in the classes they had together, Robert wasn't teasing her anymore—in fact, he was ignoring her completely. That should've felt like a good thing, but instead she felt guilty.

She sighed and turned on her cell phone. *Ding.*

Sammie hastily opened her text messages.

Come quick! Bram had written. *I think the monarch is about to hatch!*

The bus had never moved so slowly in Sammie's whole life. At the traffic lights and stops before hers, Sammie whispered under her breath, "Hurry, hurry, *hurry!*"

When the bus pulled up to Sammie's stop, she flew out so fast that she almost tripped on the bottom step. She ran the short distance home to get her bike.

Soon, with a stitch in her side and legs aching, gasping for breath, she zoomed into Bram's driveway. She dumped her bike without ceremony. She didn't even knock.

She bounded upstairs and joined Bram and his mom, who were bent over the counter in the kitchen. They'd brought the cage inside. "You're just in time, Sammie!" said Vicky.

"When I got home, I could see the outline of the wing through the chrysalis case," said Bram. He and Sammie had read that when the wings showed, the butterfly would be ready to emerge. "Thank goodness you're not too late."

The chrysalis had cracked open at the very bottom. Already a tiny black head was poking out. "Here it comes!" whispered Bram.

The creature wiggled. Then it squirmed, and the chrysalis split all the way open. The butterfly came out in a rush. With slender black legs, it clung to the chrysalis, now a clear shell hanging from the wood.

Clickety-clickety-clickety-click went Bram's camera,

capturing the moments for them to add to their symposium project.

The butterfly swung awkwardly, fumbling to get a grip on the slippery chrysalis. Sammie held her breath. Would it fall? Then the tiny black claws on the ends of its legs hooked against the ribs of the chrysalis, and the butterfly stopped wildly teetering and clung comfortably.

Its black body was thickened and huge. Its patterned wings were shrunken and crumpled like a folded-up parachute. Now, Sammie knew, it had to pump fluid from its body into its wings. It was happening fast. Already the wings were stretching out.

"It's a male," said Bram. "Look. It has the dark dots on its bottom stripes."

They watched fascinated for about ten minutes as the wings reached their proper size, folded neatly above the butterfly's back. Its previously fluid-swollen body had become slender. Its antennae waved gently, testing the air.

"I remember this from when I was a kid," said Vicky a little dreamily. "It's been so many years."

"I didn't know you raised monarchs!" said Sammie.

"Neither did I, Mom," said Bram, surprise all over his face. "You never told me about that!"

"Well, I wanted to let you and Sammie do your own thing, sweetheart. But one time, yes, I did." Vicky smiled. "I liked art already, and I went on a butterfly painting kick for a while because they are so colorful. My art teacher suggested I could draw one as it hatched. I think he wanted to give me a challenge. I wonder where those old sketches went."

Sammie tried to imagine Vicky as a little girl. It wasn't so hard. The memories made Vicky's face look younger.

"I remember it takes a while before the butterfly dries and starts moving around," Vicky added. "You could probably hold it."

Gingerly Bram unlatched the mesh lid of the cage. He hesitated. Then he turned to Sammie.

"I'm scared I'll hurt it," he said. "You're always picking up bugs. You first."

With utmost delicacy, Sammie reached under the lid. She nudged the monarch's front feet with a careful forefinger. Finding something at its knees, the monarch took one faltering step, then another, and another, until all its legs rested on Sammie's skin.

Clickety-clickety-clickety-click.

She couldn't think of anything more beautiful.

The monarch stood so lightly, she could almost imagine it wasn't there. She could just feel the little feet at the ends of its threadlike legs on her finger pad. From this close, she could see the black fuzz covering its head and body. The long, slender antennae. The brilliant wings, spotted and striped with black on orange. As Sammie held it, the butterfly opened its wings once and closed them again.

"It's your turn, Bram. You can do it."

Gently Sammie transferred the monarch onto his finger. Then he passed it to his mom. Finally, Vicky let the fragile creature crawl back into the butterfly house, which Bram clasped closed once again.

They reported its emergence to the Monarch Larva Monitoring Project website. *Adult monarch*, they proudly selected from the drop-down menu.

Most monarchs, they read, hatch in the morning, so they have time to dry during the day. But some—like theirs—do emerge in the afternoon. It was like their monarch had waited for them, Sammie thought, just so they could witness this moment.

"Looks like you'll have to wait till tomorrow to release it, so its wings can dry," Vicky said. "I can drive you two to school, if you like."

"So we can meet at Winghaven first thing!" exclaimed Bram.

Sammie nodded. "And set it free."

Early the next day, the two of them stood solemnly at the top of the Hillock, mesh cage in hand.

Winghaven looked especially golden in the morning light. The day's first sunrays slanted through thick wildflowers and made the grasses shine. *Plenty of nectar to feed our butterfly,* thought Sammie.

Bram held out the cage. Sammie lifted her arms in ceremony.

"Carry the memory of us all the way to Mexico, little monarch." She swallowed hard. "I hope you make it there."

Bram opened the cage. At first the butterfly did nothing. Then Sammie reached in and poked gently at its feet.

The butterfly fluttered nervously, batting against Sammie's hand. Then it launched itself out of the cage.

They watched it sail over Winghaven. It teetered up and down in the air, then made a sudden beeline into the thick growth and vanished.

At last they released their held breaths.

"We did it," said Bram. "Now it can travel south."

"I sure hope it survives, Bram."

For a moment they stood silently, considering the long journey ahead of their small visitor. Sammie felt a lump in her throat. They'd spent so much care and effort tending the small caterpillar, then watching over the pupa.

Sometimes the smallest things are the strongest, she remembered Bram saying.

Now it was up to their butterfly to protect itself against the huge world.

WEATHER: Thin clouds, hazy sun, no wind
LOCATION: Winghaven
TIME: 4:00 p.m.

Most people think of November as plain. No more autumn yellows and oranges and reds. But I know there's more to November than gray.

The grasses are yellow brown. A bit of green crabgrass at the bottom. At the tips of the stems are sprays of seeds.
They make the field look like a painter smudged her paint and left it all dusty.

Plus there are the milkweeds. Dark brown, split-open seedpods. They look like dark brown canoes setting off into the air.

Starlike white seeds tumble over the fields.

Go plant yourselves and make more milkweeds for the monarchs, little seeds.

Robins are clucking in the bushes. They're starting to flock for winter. Some of them migrate south. But some stay all winter to eat the red berries on the bushes.

Burnt sienna. Russet. Red. Taupe. Yellow. Burgundy. All the colors in my crayon box belong to November.

29

INVITATIONS

Winter came early. It locked itself cold and forbidding around the tall house where Sammie lived. She stared out the window at the snow, waiting for Bram.

Lately she hadn't spent much time at Winghaven. The snow was too deep to easily walk in. Besides, it got dark so early now. When Sammie got home, dusk was falling. She hadn't seen much of Bram, either, and neither of them had seen Pete in weeks.

Bram had time today, though, to meet up and work on their project. Sammie's mom was home early, so Vicky was coming over for a cup of tea.

"They're here!" yelled Sammie as Vicky's Honda pulled up to the driveway. She ran outside to meet them.

"Sammie, shut that door!" shouted her mom. "And grab the mail!"

"Hey, Sammie!" said Bram, jumping out of the car.

She grinned. "Go ahead in," she said. "My mom's got banana bread in the kitchen." She trotted down the snowy drive.

On the very top of a thick pile of junk mail, an envelope caught her eye.

It read *Samantha Tabitha Smith*, followed by her address.

A letter! For her?

She never got letters.

She stared at it. That looked an awful lot like Pete's handwriting.

She stuffed the letter into her back pocket and hurried inside.

Sammie's mom was already serving tea. Vicky sat at the big wooden table, smiling. "Your kitchen is so much cozier and more welcoming than ours, Susan," she said.

"I'm glad you like it." Sammie's mom glanced around, seeming surprised but pleased, then cut four thick slices of still-hot banana bread. "It's been harder to keep it that way, what with work."

"You keep all the balls in the air so well," said Vicky admiringly. She put her cheek in her hand with sigh. "Ever since Wesley and I moved from Seattle, I've felt like I'm scrambling to figure things out. It's so different here."

Sammie had never thought before about her mom being someone to admire.

"Let's talk about it." Her mom handed Bram and Sammie their slices. "These two are probably going to disappear straight upstairs to work as usual."

They were already fidgeting impatiently to get started. Sammie's mom's banana bread, though, was worth staying for.

Vicky smiled over the rim of her cup. "We're all excited to see this symposium project. When's the big reveal?"

"Not yet," said Sammie secretively.

Then the two of them bolted down their banana bread and slipped away to the Science Room.

It held an icy chill today from the roof's lack of insulation. Sammie turned on the small space heater.

They'd pooled their allowance money and bought big sheets of poster board. They were mounting all their photographs, drawings, and writings, framed with squares of colored paper.

The monarch poster was the centerpiece. It was almost done. It showed their plots and graphs and caterpillar photos and drawings. Sammie had written descriptions of the monarch life cycle. They had photos and descriptions of the monarch they'd raised, too.

Besides that, they were making posters of Winghaven's whole ecology. They wanted to make sure viewers understood that Winghaven wasn't just monarchs. Without the plants and birds and animals, there wouldn't even be a Field:

birds reseeded the grasses and flowers, deer nibbled away shrubs and saplings, withered plants and animal scat fertilized the soil each fall for the next year. Everything was connected.

Finally, they were preparing boxes of specimens: Sammie's milk snake skin, the one she'd found under the door; insect husks; a sun-bleached deer hoof bone Pete had untangled from the grasses; a single monarch wing Bram found on the path. And, of course, the empty pupa from the butterfly they had raised themselves.

But before they got back to work, Sammie tugged the envelope out of her back pocket, a little crumpled now. The stamp had an illustration of a heron labeled AUDUBON'S BIRDS. "Look what just turned up in the mail."

Bram raised his eyebrows. "Open it!"

She hastily tore it open. They flattened the note on Sammie's desk. The letter read

Dear Sammie and Bram,

Here's the announcement for the Audubon Society Christmas Bird Count this year. I can't think of a better pair of partners to try to spot the most birds. I bet we'll crush the other teams. The count is on December 28. We'll have to wake up before dawn. Make sure your parents know the date.

—Pete

Pete had enclosed the Audubon Society announcement. It listed the towns where the count would be held, including their own, circled by Pete's black pen. At five p.m., all the birders were invited to a local nature sanctuary for a spaghetti dinner and the bird tally.

They pounded downstairs to show their moms.

"You lucky kids!" exclaimed Vicky.

"Sounds like it'll be a great day," Sammie's mom agreed.

"Susan, I have an idea," said Vicky. *I have an idea.* Sammie had to smile at how similar Bram and his mom were. "Why don't you and Dave come over for dinner while the kids are at the tally? That'll give Dave and Wes a chance to get to know each other better. Pete can drop the kids off when they're done, and we'll all get to hear about the count."

And Susan and Vicky began laying out plans for the meal as eagerly as if they, too, were eleven years old and talking about cardboard and specimens instead of roast chicken, brussels sprouts, and apple crumble.

30

THE BIG DAY

Sammie woke before her alarm went off. Outside, the world was black. She hastily checked her bedside clock: 4:50 a.m. Still plenty of time.

Just a few days after Christmas, the Big Day had arrived at last.

Jumping out of bed, Sammie reached for the fleece hat she'd gotten as a present from her dad. And the pack of survival chocolate and hand warmers for winter treks. That was from Bram. She'd gotten him a pair of gloves with special fingertips that let him still use his camera.

She hurried downstairs to eat breakfast and wait at the front door.

When Pete's beat-up car pulled up at 5:45 a.m., her mom was only just awake, shuffling around in her slippers and bathrobe. She smiled sleepily, pouring coffee. "I don't know how a daughter of mine manages to wake up so early, honey," she said. "You have your warm socks on?"

"Yes, Mom," said Sammie.

"Long underwear?"

"Yes, Mom. I've got to go," said Sammie.

"Okay, honey. Have fun today."

Sammie was already half out the door. Pete and Bram were grinning at her from the long front seat of Pete's old station wagon. Sammie hopped in next to Bram and pulled on her seat belt.

"Ready to go?" said Pete.

"Am I ever!" said Sammie.

"Well, let's get a move on! We've got to start before light."

Pete's warm car felt good after the bite of dark and snow. It smelled like the air-freshener tree hanging from his mirror.

"I've got the perfect plan," he said. "We'll cover some special haunts I know around here in the morning and save Winghaven for the afternoon. We'll start at the pond at the big hotel on Split Road."

"Won't it be frozen?" said Bram.

"Questions, questions!" said Pete. "You'll see."

In the hotel parking lot, they hopped out after Pete into air that froze Sammie's nostrils. "The hour before dawn is always the coldest," Pete remarked. "That's when the earth has lost the most heat from the day before."

By now, the darkness had turned furry gray. "Look," said Pete.

Many small black bodies, even blacker than the early dawn, were moving on the pond. Sammie could hear them softly quacking and honking.

"There must be hundreds of them out there!" said Bram.

"This pond never freezes," said Pete. "That's the secret. The hotel's underground pipes warm it up. It's the only open water for miles around."

"So the ducks and geese come to spend the night!" Sammie said.

Pete nodded. "When the sun comes up, they'll fly away to look for food. First, we'll get to count them and check for any rare ducks."

They counted eighty-five mallards and forty-one Canada geese. Among them, they also spotted a pintail, a duck with a long, long tail like a needle and a curved white streak down its neck that Bram said looked like a bass clef in sheet music. As they climbed back into the car, Pete high-fived them. "No one else will have that species," he said.

Streaks of pink and gold and silver filled up the sky as they rolled on to the next stop.

Pete knew where to find *everything*. They stopped next at

the small airfield on Brown Boulevard. "Look for something gray," he said.

At first, nothing stirred. Sammie stared through her binoculars as though her eyes were stuck open. They found some ordinary birds—a field sparrow and a flock of winter robins. Sammie dutifully wrote them down.

"There." Pete spotted it first.

They peered through their binoculars at a distant pale shape. "A mockingbird?" said Bram in some confusion. "What's special about that?"

Pete chuckled. "Look closer." He unfolded his spotting scope—an instrument like a small telescope on a tripod—and the two kids looked through.

A northern shrike! Neither Sammie nor Bram had ever seen one. Pete said he'd never managed to score a shrike on bird count day. He'd found it a few days earlier, and luckily it was still hanging around. It sat hunched on a branch like a little wizard: gray, with black eyes and a hooked beak, no bigger than a blue jay. Shrikes, Pete said, eat grasshoppers and bugs in the summer, but in winter they catch mice.

The birders were hungry before eleven a.m. and took a break to eat. For lunch they sat in Pete's car and had peanut butter and jelly sandwiches. Sammie passed out chocolate. Pete shared his thermos of hot cocoa. "Cold makes a body hungry," he said.

They counted their species so far. Sammie was keeping the list. "Twenty-three," she said. "Is that good?"

"As good as I've ever had by this time," said Pete. "Not good enough, though. Good thing we've got our secret plan for the afternoon."

Winghaven, thought Sammie impatiently.

At last they rolled up to the entry path and hopped out.

In Winghaven, they knew just where to look. They found all the birds they were hoping for: a ruffed grouse; a snipe; even a merlin, shaped like a peregrine falcon but tiny and brown, coasting overhead. Their list was getting long. Sammie stared at it with pride. "Forty-eight," she said.

They finished the northern part of Winghaven, taking their time to stalk all the way to the Pond along the snowy path already tamped down by deer. In the southern part, clouds of horned larks, snow buntings, and song sparrows blew along the furrows between grasses bent by snow.

When they reached the stone wall, Bram stared off to the right. "The Junkyard House sure looks different in winter," he said.

"I don't know why you're so interested in that place," said Sammie.

"There might be a good bird or two down there," said Bram.

Turning off the path, he again slogged downhill toward the decaying clapboard house. "Bram!" Sammie called, trying to keep her voice quiet but audible. She hung close to Pete as Bram's figure half vanished down the slope. "Come back."

"Wait," Bram called. "Something's been going on down here." They could see only his head now—just enough of him to know he'd raised his camera to snap a few photos.

A muffled warning bark from within the house sounded into the quiet winter air. Bram came scrambling back, waving his equipment triumphantly. "Check this out," he said.

They bent over his screen.

Around the Junkyard House, deep dents had been pressed into the snowy ground by heavy machinery, leaving churned-up scars in the soil below. The broken-down cars and trash that had once marred the yard were gone.

"I thought their stuff was hidden by snow, but they actually hauled it all away!" said Bram. "And the for sale sign is gone."

"I guess they cleaned up their yard to get their house sold," said Pete. "Maybe the next folks will be a little neater, huh?"

Sammie took a deep breath and checked her notebook page. "Fifty-four," she said.

"Really good," said Pete. "But still not good enough. Let's keep cracking on."

Finally evening began to steal over the snowy field. On the horizon, a huge moon was rising in the dusk against a fading sky. They had a half hour left before the tally.

Pete still wasn't satisfied. He rubbed his long hands together to warm them up. "I want one more species," he said. "Just one more. That'll put me five species higher than I've ever had. If we wait a few more minutes, we could get lucky."

Sammie stamped and blew on her hands. She was freezing. And hungry, too. She wanted to ask if they could go and get their spaghetti, but a scientist wouldn't give up just like that.

"Let's try this," Pete said.

He cupped his hands around his mouth and hooted.

The sound rang out over the woods, a deep *"Hoo! Hoo! Hoo!"* It sounded eerie in the darkening light.

"It's great horned owl season," Pete murmured. "They set up territories in December and January. I don't want to hoot too much, or I might disturb them. Let's wait. One might come."

They waited.

And one did.

A huge pale shape floated out of the woodland like a

ghost. It landed on a branch of a bare tree. Its silhouette against the sky showed two tufts of feathers sticking up from its head like horns.

Then it dropped down from the branch and flew right over their heads, its big wings beating noiselessly in the frosty air. It vanished into the woods across the Field.

Sammie let out her breath, and all three of them burst out laughing with sheer happiness.

"We *got* one!" said Pete. "I just knew we would. *Now* we can head to the official gathering."

Joyfully they tramped back up the snowy path. Pete dug through his pockets for his keys.

Sammie gazed tiredly around as Pete unlocked the doors. She was sleepy and half-frozen. Her feet felt like blocks of ice. Then she noticed a tiny blob on a wire above.

"Hey, what's that?"

It was pressed up against a telephone pole. Pete and Bram leaned forward, trying to make it out. The light was almost gone, replaced by moonglow. But there sat a tiny feathered creature with a rounded head. A screech owl. It was as small as a fist.

They gazed at it a long time, whispering in delight. Once or twice, it turned its head like on a pivot. It looked right at them, but it didn't seem to mind that they were there. Finally, they left it still staring out into the dusk.

Pete twitched and fidgeted in his seat as he drove. "I've never had such a great bird count day, never!" he kept saying. "Fifty-six! Wow!"

"Do you think we'll win the count?" said Bram.

"We've got to," said Pete. "After a day like today, we just do!"

WEATHER: Cold! Below freezing (25°F)
LOCATION: THE BIG DAY!
TIME: 5:45 a.m.

<u>Starting location: Hotel Pond, Split Road</u>
  Canada Goose (CANG): 41
  Northern Pintail (NOPI): 1 (!)

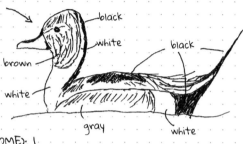

  Hooded Merganser (HOME): 1
  Black Duck (ABDU): 14
  Herring Gull (HERG): 21+7 (airfield)
  Ring-billed Gull (RBGU): 11
  House Sparrow (HOSP): 22+ ʜʜ
                   +15 (airfield)
  Cardinal (NOCA): 1
  Pigeon (ROPI): 26
  Starling (EUST): 15+40 (airfield)
  Mallard (MALL): 85+2 (airfield, flying)

<u>In woods near hotel:</u>
  Chickadee (BCCH): 10
  Downy Woodpecker (DOWO): 11 11
  Blue Jay (BLJA): 11 1
  White-breasted
    Nuthatch (WBNU): 2
  Brown Creeper (BRCR): 1

<u>8:00 a.m. Airfield on Brown Boulevard</u>
  Field Sparrow (FISP): 1
  American Robin (AMRO): 25
  Northern Shrike (!)(NSHR): 1
  Red-tailed Hawk (RTHA): 1
  Crows (AMCR): ʜʜ ʜʜ 111
  Song Sparrow (SOSP): 111

<u>Later, flying over the car:</u>
  Bald Eagle (BAEA): 1

10:45 a.m
Early lunch—we are
  starved. Now on
  to Winghaven!

31

LOSS

The Audubon building was long and wooden with big beams overhead. It smelled like pine and wood smoke. And spaghetti.

Tables, big and round and made of oak, filled the room. On one side stood a display of stuffed animal skins—a porcupine and a squirrel and a coyote. Sammie felt sorry for them. Pete said they'd been there for years. He said naturalists used to shoot animals to study them up close. Now, he said, scientists are more interested in learning animals' habits in their environments.

On one table, a piggy bank and a stack of pledge cards stood next to a sign: FUNDRAISER FOR LAND CONSERVATION. "Our land-purchase fund has shrunk as economic shifts have slowed charitable giving," it read. "The region is growing, and development is spreading. Many areas of natural land are now at risk. Please consider a donation!"

I sure hope they don't mean Winghaven, thought Sammie, remembering what Robert had said. But she stayed silent. Saying it out loud seemed like a bad omen.

They pooled their change to make a dollar and dropped it in.

As she and Bram stood by the table, Pete half loped over to them with his long-legged stride. He was followed by a slender, strong-looking woman with gray hair pulled back in a ponytail. Her eyes gleamed like a hare in the underbrush. Sammie liked her right away.

"Sammie and Bram, this is Jean Sand," said Pete. "She's the director of this branch of the Audubon Society."

Sammie felt shy immediately, but Jean smiled warmly as they each shook her hand. "What a pleasure to meet you both," she said. "I've heard so much about this pair of young naturalists."

"You'll see what experts they are once we sit down for the bird count," said Pete, beaming his crooked-toothed smile.

"I can't wait," said Jean. "Now you should all hurry to get some food before it's gone."

"Hardly a chance of that!" said Pete. "You planned for an army."

They followed Jean into the line and heaped their plates. Sammie had never seen someone fit as much food on one plate as Pete did. He had to make a pyramid with his meat-balls to fit them all.

"How do you stay so skinny when you eat so much?" one of the other birders asked him.

"Oh, I keep busy," said Pete. "Just you wait. You'll see when the count starts."

"Pete, you say that every year, but you've never won!" said the other birder, teasing.

Pete just grinned. Then he leaned over and whispered in Sammie's ear, "Yeah, but last year I didn't have my wood sprites for helpers."

The count leader called everyone together. He had on canvas pants and huge boots.

First the leader went around the room species by species, to tally how many birds of each species had been seen. Pete said that helped show if any given bird was struggling to survive.

"Crows!" called out the count leader.

Every team answered, one at a time.

"Fifty."

"Twenty-four."

"A hundred thirty-five."

"A thousand and one."

"Wow!" Sammie whispered to Pete. "How'd they get so many crows?"

"The town dump's in their zone," Pete whispered back. "The crows roost there in the winter. That's the Southwest group—the most likely to beat us on the total species number."

Some kinds of bird no one had seen. And others only one or two groups had spotted.

"Iceland gull," said the group leader.

"One!" someone called out. Southwest again.

"Dang," said Pete. "Last year I got one of those. We didn't get one this year."

"It's okay," Bram whispered. "We've got the owls."

"Shhh," replied Pete, eyes shining with glee. "Don't give it away before our moment."

The count droned on and on. Sammie felt ready to burst. Bram was trying to keep track of every other team's total species as they listed off their bird numbers. Eventually, he admitted he'd lost count.

"Great horned owl," said the group leader. There was a silence. Pete poked Sammie.

"One!" she said.

"Wow!" said the leader, checking it off. Everyone murmured in surprise. He listed off two more owls. Then . . .

"Screech owl," he said.

Again silence spread. Bram grinned at Pete. Pete nudged him. "Go on."

"One!" called Bram.

Again everyone murmured in pleasure.

"You're the owl team!" said the leader, smiling. "Great job. We haven't had any owls since three years ago. You must've birded some great habitat."

They exchanged glances, eyes glowing with pride.

"Okay," the leader finally said. "Now to see who's got the most different species this year."

Sammie sucked in her breath. Pete looked confident, but Sammie wasn't so sure—Southwest had so many birds.

"East!" called the leader.

"Thirty-six," they said. Sammie sighed with relief. They were no competition.

"Forty-one," said the next group, North.

"Forty-eight," said West, a group Bram had said he thought was doing pretty well.

Then it was their turn. "Southeast," said the leader.

"You do it," said Pete to Sammie.

"Fifty-six!" she said. There was a murmur of surprise in the room.

"That's remarkable!" put in Jean Sand, who'd been listening from the side, leaning back with her jean-clad legs outstretched. "I can't remember the last time a team had so many."

Sammie, Pete, and Bram grinned nervously at one another. But there was one group left.

"Southwest," said the leader.

Everyone looked at them. Their team's announcer took a deep breath. "Fifty . . ." she said. You could have heard a pin drop. Sammie's heart stopped. No. They couldn't have beaten them. They couldn't!

". . . four."

Sammie and Bram leaped out of their seats. "Hooray!" shouted Sammie. She hugged Pete around the neck as hard as she could. "You did it, Pete!"

"I didn't do it!" said Pete. He looked so proud. "We did."

Just before they went home, Jean Sand walked up to them. "You were right about this pair," she said to Pete. "They're already impressive naturalists. We'd be more than happy to have both of you take part in our science symposium this spring. They'll be our first student team ever."

Bram and Sammie looked at each other in delight but did what they could to keep a veneer of calm. Bram straightened his shoulders and reached to shake Jean's hand. "It's really an honor," he said courteously. "Thank you so much."

Sammie felt proud of how professional Bram looked and sounded.

"I look forward to seeing your work," Jean said, smiling, and stepped away.

The moment Jean was out of earshot, Bram danced a little caper before high-fiving Sammie.

"Hooray!" they both burst out. And then both of them high-fived Pete.

After the bird count, Pete drove them home. Sammie leaned sleepily against the window. The moon was washing the whole world with silver. Every branch, every needle glistened on the trees. They seemed to reflect the glow of the evening at the Audubon count.

After a few minutes of quiet driving, Pete spoke up. "So," he said. "I have some news."

Bram was sitting in the middle. "Oh yeah?" he said. "Good news?"

"Well, yes and no," said Pete. He took a deep breath. "I'm glad you two were able to join me today, because this is a celebration of sorts. A goodbye celebration."

The inside of the car suddenly seemed very quiet. "What do you mean?"

"I'm moving away."

Sammie went cold. "You're what? Pete, you can't leave!"

"I got a really amazing job. It's in Washington, DC, the capital. It'll be a chance to really help make a difference for animals and the outdoors. I won't get to work outside as much as I do now. I'll be talking with politicians and writing memos a lot of the time—but it's an important career move for me."

"Man, oh man," said Bram, "we're going to miss you, Pete. It won't be the same without you."

Sammie's heart beat at the bottom of her stomach. No more Pete. After their perfect day and now in this perfect night of moon and snow, it felt unreal.

"How come you didn't tell us before?" she said.

"I only found out three days ago," said Pete. "I didn't want to spoil our Big Day with sad news. I'm leaving in a couple weeks."

"A couple weeks," repeated Bram. "That's really soon."

"But . . . but what about the symposium?" wailed Sammie. "You'll miss it!"

"You two are as ready as you can possibly be to present your work, kiddo. You don't need me anymore. You're real naturalists now, you know? You've blasted right past me like rocket ships." He grinned at them. Still, his long, doglike face looked sadder than normal—it didn't squinch up as much as it usually did when he smiled.

"Don't go, Pete," said Sammie, swallowing her tears. "Find another job here."

"Come on, Sammie." Bram lightly punched her knee, his brows creased. "This is good news for Pete. Congratulations, Pete."

For some reason he was staring at her instead of Pete,

keenly watching her, when she was hardly the one who mattered right now.

She couldn't bring herself to get the word *congratulations* past the lump in her throat. She nodded.

Pete pulled into the driveway of Bram's house. They sat silently for a moment. Then Pete reached out one long, long arm around both their shoulders and gave them a squeeze.

"You two are one reason I'm sad to go," he said. "You're my team. Don't forget it."

Sammie and Bram climbed out of Pete's car. They turned and watched the battered red station wagon back out of the drive, tires crunching softly against remnant snow. Pete's shadowy figure waved one last time through the window, silhouetted by moonlight. They lifted their mittened hands in response, and his car pulled away, its lights disappearing down the hill.

They walked slowly up to the front door, side by side. Bram opened it. A golden light spilled onto the snow.

A burst of laughter floated down the stairs. Sammie and Bram pulled off their coats and boots and made their way up. Their parents were still sitting around the dining room table. They were talking and laughing. Wineglasses and dessert plates glinted. Despite her sadness at losing Pete, Sammie had to smile. Their parents were getting along as well as she and Bram did.

"Aha, it's our young adventurers!" exclaimed Bram's dad. "How did it go?"

"We won!" said Bram. "Fifty-six species of birds!"

"Wow!" A hubbub began. Parents asking questions. Bram, mostly, answering, telling the story of their day. Sammie listened, adding a detail or two that Bram had forgotten.

Pete. Pete was going away. Who would they tell when they spotted a particularly amazing bird? Who would help them think up their next ecosystem study?

"Are you okay, Sammie? You're awfully quiet." Vicky looked down with gentle concern. "Would you like some dessert?"

Sammie shook her head. Her mom leaned over to feel her forehead. Sammie pulled back to avoid the touch.

"It's late," said her dad. "Cold weather wears kids out."

Everyone got up from the table. The chairs scraped against the wooden floor.

"Run and get your coat on, Sammie."

Sammie trudged obediently to the landing and began pulling on her boots. As she did, she heard her own name. Her mother and Vicky were talking in quiet tones. Gossip. About her. She paused and pricked up her ears.

"Sammie's been a different person since meeting Bram," she heard her mother say. "So much more confident and mature."

"They've been wonderful for each other," said Vicky. "Bram was devastated to leave Seattle. His old school had a self-directed learning model, and public school has been tough. Finding a friend who shares his interests has helped him adjust."

Sammie listened in surprise. *She* had helped Bram? Bram always seemed to know everything. She hadn't noticed any changes in herself. Had she really become more grown-up this year?

"Yes, they're certainly passionate about the outdoors," said her mother. "Sammie doesn't think about anything else!"

"They're quite obsessed," agreed Vicky. "Bram's always liked to throw himself into one thing. I don't think he's ever had a friend as single-minded as he is until he met Sammie."

"That's Sammie exactly," said Susan in a rueful voice.

"I was a bit like that, too, growing up," said Vicky. "Bram yearns to do things that matter. I think Sammie makes him feel needed."

"Perhaps he'll help her branch out and make new friends."

Even though Vicky's words felt good, Sammie felt a surge of irritation. She didn't want new friends. She wanted Pete and Bram and Winghaven. How come her mom still didn't understand?

She jumped up and pounded back up the stairs. "I'm ready!" she shouted.

"Goodness, Sammie, there's no need to yell!" said her mother.

"She must be tired," said Vicky, ruffling her hair. "Go get some good sleep, sweetheart."

Sammie followed her parents out the door, back into the moon-glimmering snow.

She wasn't tired, she thought.

Just sad.

32

THREAT

Snow clung in thick crusts until late March. Then with-out warning one afternoon, as Sammie stepped off the school bus, she could tell things had changed.

Moisture tingled her nose in the newly humid air. Also, the birds' songs had changed. They were no longer letting out the thin notes they used to keep contact with one another as they moved in their winter flocks. Now their voices were liquid. She heard tunes she hadn't heard all winter: a flutelike warble of a cardinal, a bright chitter of sparrows. And best of all, the mourning doves were doing their mating flight. They stretched their wings out stiff as boards in an arcing swoop, like boomerangs silhouetted against the clouds.

Sammie lifted her arms high. *It's spring!* she felt like shouting. But she was a good naturalist and didn't want to frighten any birds or animals that had waited so long for winter's end.

"It's spring," she whispered. She hurried home and turned her bicycle into the damp breeze. Soon the wind was blowing and biting against her face as she whipped down the snow-banked roads.

The Audubon symposium was at the end of the week, and she and Bram had toiled over every particle of their project until it felt right.

She raced straight for Winghaven. Bram would know to meet her there on a day like today. But the moment she arrived, she saw that something was wrong.

Gashes had been cut into the entry path's damp soil, which was soft from melted snow. They were patterned by tire tracks. Someone had driven a car through here.

Anger darted through her. Who had done this? Maybe the people from the Junkyard House had decided to bring another one of their broken-down cars this way. Surely they'd already moved away, though.

Whoever it was, maybe they were still in Winghaven now.

Keeping her footsteps as quiet as she could and clinging close to the tree line, she peeped out.

The afternoon was bright and blustery. Huge dark clouds blew across the horizon. The sun flashed out between them, painting the pines on the hill a brilliant deep green. The glitter of light made Sammie almost blind.

She let her eyes adjust from the dimness of the path.

She didn't see Bram. And she didn't see any cars. But what she did see terrified her.

All around Winghaven, bright pink flagging tape had been tied around the trunks of the trees.

Sammie's heart was hammering with unease and fear. She had to find out more.

She hurried to the closest tape. No labels or nearby string suggested someone's science research, like Pete's old site in the woods. She'd better get Bram; she was already farther into Winghaven than she was supposed to be. Together they could figure out what was going on. Where was he, anyway?

Straining her ears, she listened for any movement. She tried to push down her rising fear, but partway back, panic got the better of her. She broke into a run, racing up and out the entry path to the road.

Silly. No one was here. The entry path lay empty, vegetation pushed back, the tire tracks like scars. She composed herself and pedaled to Bram's.

She dropped her bicycle, ran up the driveway, and banged on the door. But Bram didn't answer it. Instead, Vicky came to the door.

"Is . . . is Bram here?"

Vicky looked backward into the house. She looked distracted.

"Hi, Sammie. Bram can't go out to Winghaven today, I'm

afraid. We're leaving on our family trip tonight and he needs to pack."

"Family trip?" Sammie stared at Vicky, taken aback.

"Yes, to Seattle, for just a few days. Didn't Bram tell you about that?" Vicky's tone was brusque, and she looked like she was in a hurry.

"To Seattle?" exclaimed Sammie in bewilderment. She blinked and shook her head.

Vicky looked at her, then smiled thoughtfully, looking a little more like her unstressed self. "He must not have had a chance. I'll tell him to call or send an email." Before Sammie could ask anything more, Vicky squeezed her shoulder. "We'll see you Saturday at the symposium, okay? It'll be great. Bye now." And the door closed.

Sammie stood fretting on the step. The afternoon that had started so beautifully had taken a sharp turn. She pondered a moment, then made up her mind.

This was too important to wait.

She trotted down the steps, then circled the house to where the low window opened into Bram's bedroom. She knelt on the wet soil, damp seeping in at her knees. Then she peered inside.

Bram was turned away from her, folding clothing and tucking it into a suitcase flapped open on his bed. He was working slowly, and his shoulders were hunched.

She knocked on the glass.

He looked up startled. Then he crossed the room, reached up, and unlatched the window.

"What are you doing here?" he whispered. "Didn't my mom just tell you I couldn't come out?"

"She said you're going to Seattle! What's going on?"

"I, um . . . well, my dad's going on a business trip, and my mom decided we would all go." For some reason, he wasn't meeting her eyes. "She thought . . . I guess she thought it would be nice to see Seattle again. I figured we'd be there and back so fast you wouldn't even notice I was gone."

Sammie stared at him. But she didn't have time for this now, she thought. She'd have to find out more about his trip later.

"Bram, I've got to talk to you. It can't wait," whispered Sammie. "Something bad is happening at Winghaven."

She quickly described the flagging and tire tracks she had seen.

Bram's gaze snapped up, and his eyes widened as she spoke. "Flagging tape normally means they plan to cut down the trees. I used to see it at logging sites near Seattle," he said. "I bet there's something about it online." Then he looked behind himself, hesitated, and turned back to Sammie, making a *shhh* sign against his lips with a forefinger. "My mom's really stressed, so we've got to make this fast. Do you think you can climb in?"

This felt more like normal Bram. "I can climb anything," said Sammie. Turning onto her belly, she shimmied feet first into the bedroom. The soil dirtied her jacket but she didn't care.

They turned to his desk. His laptop blinked on with a soft wheeze.

"There's nothing on the city hall website," said Bram. "There's not even an announcement in the *Herald*."

"Then why is there flagging tape?"

Bram frowned and typed in a few more searches, hunched over the computer in concentration, fingers flying.

"Hey, look at this."

On his screen was a document with hundreds of tiny listings. It was marked CITY PROPERTIES FOR SALE. "It's dated four years ago."

He pointed with his stylus to one line: UNDEVELOPED LAND, 5528–5550 SPLIT ROAD. OWNER: CITY OF WESTHAM. Next to the line had been added *Temporarily withdrawn from the market.*

"That was ages ago! And if it's gone up for sale again, wouldn't they have announced it?" Sammie said. "No one at the Audubon Society mentioned anything about it, and it seems like they would know."

"That gives me an idea," said Bram. "Maybe the Audubon Society could help stop whatever's going on. Remember they had that land-purchase fund? We should document the flagging and add it to our project to let them know." He drummed his fingers rapidly on the desk. "Darn this trip! I wish I could go with you to Winghaven and take some photos. But I only get back the evening before the symposium."

Sammie bit her lip. She didn't feel great about going back into Winghaven alone, with the unnerving tracks left in the soggy, slushy mud, not knowing whether someone sinister was in there. And it would break her promise to her mom—again.

"I can take the pictures," she said anyway.

In his older-brother voice, Bram said, "You're not supposed to go in there by yourself. You promised."

"I know. But this is an emergency," she said.

Bram studied her. Then he made up his mind. "Well, it's only once," he said. "Listen, I'll give you my camera so you get good-quality pictures. You just have to not let anything happen to it, okay? Here—I'll show you how to use it."

He grabbed his camera and whispered an explanation of the buttons. He seemed to go on and on.

"Bram?" Vicky's voice sounded from upstairs. "Are you talking to someone? I told you there's no time to hang out with Sammie this afternoon!"

They heard her footsteps approaching from the floor above.

"I'd better go," blurted Sammie. She hastily retreated to the window.

She stood on Bram's desk and squirmed back out. Bram reached up and thrust his camera into her hands.

"Good luck," he whispered. "Be careful with my camera." And then he shut the window.

33
CAMERA DIFFICULTIES

Sammie hurried straight back to Winghaven and made her way uneasily down the entry path. Bram's camera hung at her neck, weighty and intimidating.

She hiked all the way around the Field, her boots dampened by melting snow and mud. The flagging tape went on and on and on.

What about the alder thickets and the woodland next to the Pond? Had they been marked, too?

She chewed her bottom lip and gazed down the side path. This early in the season, the weeds hadn't grown yet. Faster than usual, she reached her destination.

At the Pond, to her dismay, the trees again bore the telltale pink tape. She found a big boot print in the mud of the shoreline. Fury welled up in her heart. How dare they? The boot print looked recent. She stood motionless, listening for human sounds. But all she could hear was the wind soughing through the alder groves.

She still hadn't found out much information—like what, exactly, all this flagging was for. She finally lifted the camera to her eyes and took a shot. Then she pressed the left button to see how it had turned out. The image appeared. It was blurry.

She made a face and pressed a button she guessed would take her back to the main photo screen. Instead, a menu popped up. She tried again—no luck. Frustrated, she let the camera fall to her side and walked deeper into the woods, following the trail of flags.

Suddenly she glimpsed someone sitting on the leaf litter, facing away from her. She froze.

A boy, about her age.

Bigger than her, with hunched shoulders.

She took a step backward, to escape into the woods. But at that moment, Robert turned his head, peered through the trees, and spotted her.

His expression looked sullen. "What are you doing here?" he said.

"What are *you* doing?"

"None of your business," said Robert. "You never tell me what you're up to, so why should I?"

Abruptly a rush of courage poured into Sammie from the flagged trees around her. This was Winghaven. Her place, where she'd worked and learned for so long. The threat to its landscapes woke up new resolve in her. She stood up straight and looked squarely at Robert.

"Everything in Winghaven is my business," she said. "I belong here. And I care about it."

"Well, maybe you're not the only one who can care about things," said Robert with a resentful glare.

His comment caught Sammie by surprise. She peered at him. "If you cared, you wouldn't be so mean about it maybe getting torn down soon."

Robert snorted. "I just said that to get a rise out of you," he said. "It's so easy to work you up. This place has been here forever. It'll always be here."

"That might not be true." Sammie pointed at the pink flags. "Bram and I saw online that it might have gone up for sale."

"Huh." Robert studied the flagging. "My dad's going to be pretty mad. He said he'd go into a rage if someone cut down these woods."

"Why does *he* care? He just comes in here to kill things."

"That's just what you would think," said Robert with a slight sneer. "But you're going to learn something soon. Hunters can be some of the best conservationists out there. That's what your friend Pete told me."

Sammie blinked at Robert, blank. "Pete? You met Pete?"

"Yeah. You think you're the only one who can come in here and find out about stuff, but you're wrong."

Pete. *Pete* had talked to Robert. Why hadn't he told Sammie about it? Maybe he'd thought it would upset her.

"And you think you and your boyfriend are gonna be the only kids at the Audubon Science Symposium, but you're wrong about that, too."

Sammie felt light-headed. "You . . . you're going to the Audubon symposium?"

"Yeah. Pete told me I should make a project about hunting and wilderness protection. He said it would be good for people to understand the connection. He showed me how to use his old camera and said I should take some pictures of the animals we usually shoot."

Before anger at Pete's betrayal could replace Sammie's shock, Robert spoke again.

"He said I should tell you myself. But I didn't." For the first time Robert looked away. He looked embarrassed. "So don't get mad at him about it."

Sammie's thoughts were reeling.

Robert couldn't have talked to Pete more than a few times. But he already seemed as attached to Pete as she and Bram were. Somehow Pete had won Robert over instantly, just like he had with Sammie.

Her curiosity got the better of her. "Can I see your photos?"

"Get lost, Snob Girl," he snapped. "You don't want me around, so scram."

Maybe Robert hadn't changed after all. Sammie frowned and turned away. With Winghaven in trouble, she shouldn't be wasting brain space on him anyway.

"Wait," Robert called out. She turned back in surprise. "Look, I told you what *I'm* doing—now you tell me what you're doing."

She eyed Robert for a long, long moment. "I'm trying to take pictures of this flagging," she said. "So we can let the Audubon Society know what's going on. But I can't get Bram's camera to work."

Robert shrugged. "It's not that hard. Give it to me."

Be careful with my camera, Bram had said.

Could she trust Robert? Wouldn't he just run off with it, or break it on purpose?

This is an emergency, she'd said. And it was. She needed these photos. Slowly, reluctantly, she stepped forward. "Don't hurt it," she said. "It's not mine."

He stood up off the wet ground and took it from her hands. Then he turned it to show her.

"Look. See this knob? Just put it on this setting. A for 'Auto.' Then the camera will take care of all the details."

"I couldn't even get to the main menu," admitted Sammie.

Robert actually chuckled. "Here I thought you were so smart."

Sammie's head snapped up. But for once Robert didn't look mean. He sounded like Bram when he was teasing her.

He showed her a couple more buttons to press. He knew much less about the camera than Bram, but that meant he only showed her what she could handle. Then he lifted the camera and took a picture of the woods and the scraps of pink flagging. "There. That won't be a great shot 'cause the trees are all mushed together, so it doesn't give the right idea. But at least you've got one. You can get a better photo up in the field bit where you usually hang out."

"That's . . . that's actually super nice of you, Robert." She couldn't hide the surprise in her voice. He'd never, ever been kind to her, not once. "Thanks."

Robert shrugged. "Whatever."

"I'd better go," she said.

"Yeah." Robert clutched his camera—Pete's own old one—closer. "See ya, Snob Girl." He turned away, looking unfriendly again. "Don't forget to get plenty of help from your parents on your project so it can be better than mine." Then he stomped off through the woods.

Stung, Sammie trudged back toward the Pond with drawn brows. Who did Robert think she was? These days she hardly ever got help from her parents. They were too busy and stressed out. Anyway, she'd always preferred doing things for herself.

It really was time to get home. The woodland gave way to alders, still leafless but thicker and thicker as Sammie went on. She'd missed the Pond somehow and ended up somewhere in the alder grove she and Bram had struggled through the first time she'd invited him into Winghaven. Battling nets of thin whippy trees, she tried to aim her footsteps back toward the Field. She glanced worriedly at the time. What with bumping into Robert, she was running really late.

At last she could see a gap, an end to the thicket. Finally. She shoved through a last mesh of clinging branches.

A rectangle of muddy lawn met her eyes.

She was in the backyard of the Junkyard House.

34

FROM BAD TO WORSE

How had she gotten so off track? The alders had turned her all around.

It would take forever to get back through the alders now. She would just quickly cut through the Junkyard House's backyard, she resolved.

Three steps in and the quiet was shattered.

Without warning, barking maniacally, a dog was at her elbow, a huge, lanky Irish setter, red and shaggy, with bared teeth. Its eyes were wild, the whites showing. Hysteria rang in its voice. Sammie froze, terrorized, one arm upraised protectively around Bram's camera.

Sammie gasped, "It's okay, doggy." But the barking drowned her out.

Jumping and dancing in front of her, the dog bumped the top of its head against her lifted arm. Startled, it whipped its head around—and bit down hard on her wrist.

Sammie cried out and wrenched her arm away, the camera thumping down against her side. In the same motion, she turned and ran, clutching her bitten wrist. Her breath sobbed in her chest as she raced up the slope to Winghaven.

Behind her the dog's wild barking stopped. The familiar main path of Winghaven was under her feet at last. She kept running, her breath scraping, her heart knocking her rib cage. She flung a look backward.

The dog wasn't following her.

She paused, gasping, hand still clutched around her wrist. Frightened of what she would see, Sammie uncurled her good hand from around her aching bitten one.

Four marks showed where the dog's incisors had torn her skin. The dog had caught the side of her wrist in a glancing bite. Angry red scrapes spoke of other sharp teeth besides the incisors. But the bleeding was slight, the marks shallow. It wasn't a bad wound.

Sammie's knees turned to water. She sank down to sit on the path. Then, in a mix of relief and fear and anger at her stupidity, she burst into tears.

After a minute or two, her sobs slowed. She took a shuddering breath. There was no use crying about it. She'd been bitten by a dog. Now it was over. She stared her wrist.

People these days had to get their dogs vaccinated for rabies, she thought. And she was pretty sure dogs didn't give you any other diseases. She would be fine. She wouldn't let her parents find out about this.

She looked Bram's camera over, hoping she hadn't damaged it. It seemed okay.

It was awkward to ride her bicycle with one arm. But she managed it. At home she slithered like a weasel past her mom cooking in the kitchen and ran upstairs to the bathroom. She washed her wrist, pulled down a bottle of peroxide from the medicine cabinet, and poured a bit over the wound. It stung. She gritted her teeth and bore it. That should kill any microbes, she thought. She went to her bedroom and put on a clean shirt long enough to hide the bandage.

That night, Sammie lay wide awake in bed. She tried to sense if she didn't feel well. If she might be stiffening up. She felt light-headed. But maybe that was because she was scared. She tossed and turned in bed, feeling very alone with her fears. She hadn't been able to reach Bram, and his silence made her feel even worse.

Come on, she willed herself. *Fall asleep!* But she kept imagining how awful her parents would feel if she caught rabies. She'd read about it online. Once symptoms started, it was usually too late to save someone. Finally, in an agony of worry, she leaped out of bed. Better to give away her secret than to die horribly.

She could hear her mother, still awake, brushing her teeth in the downstairs bathroom.

Sammie padded down the steps barefoot. Then, heart pounding, she knocked on the bathroom door. "Mom?"

"Come in, honey," said her mom.

Sammie opened the door. "Mom," she started. "I need to talk to you."

Then she burst into tears.

35

DISCOVERIES

The next day, Sammie's mom kept her home from school. She packed her into the car. Then they zoomed along the town streets to Split Road.

Sammie had expected to get in trouble. Instead, her mom had turned all business.

"The first thing is to make sure that dog is vaccinated," her mom said, her forehead creased with worry. "I knew I had a bad feeling about that place. But what's done is done."

Slowly they bumped up the dirt road leading to the Junkyard House. Sammie had never entered this way. As they pulled into the house's front drive, she stared uncomfortably, seeing it through her mom's eyes. The paint peeling on its walls. The broken gutter, the window sash half off its hinges. At least the cars that had moldered in the yard, collapsed and rusting, were gone.

They got out. Everything was quiet. No sound of a dog

barking. No one coming out to see who had driven up. The silence was so total it was eerie.

Sammie's mom walked straight to the front door without hesitation. She knocked. Then she knocked harder. Nothing.

"No one home," said her mom in a tight voice.

"Mom," squeaked Sammie.

She pointed to a sign stuck in the soil: UNDER CONTRACT.

Sammie's mom pursed her lips. Then she waded right into the bed of shrubs at the side of the house. She stood on tiptoes and peered through a downstairs window.

Normally Sammie couldn't imagine her mom walking through someone's flower bed, much less looking into their window.

"There's nothing in there," said her mother. "No furniture. Nothing. They've gone."

"Oh," gulped Sammie.

"Of all the bad luck," said her mother. "They must have left yesterday. Or maybe they were stopping back through when their dog bit you." She paused, thinking, shoes half-sunk in soil.

"We'll go to city hall," she declared. "We might be able to find out how to contact them."

Her mother was behaving like a little soldier: when one line of attack failed, she set off immediately on another. A small piece of Sammie couldn't help savoring her mom being so focused on her again, even while feeling guilty about it. Taking a day off work for Sammie was a big deal for her mom—she never did that these days.

City hall loomed, a big brick building with an imposing gold eagle perched on top. Her mother was soon bending over records with a city clerk, deep in conversation. Sammie waited on a hall bench, staring at the hallway's cold, dreary black tiles.

Next to the city clerk's office, she noticed another door: PLANNING AND LAND USE DEPARTMENT.

Maybe even in disgrace and at risk of death, she could find out something useful. She hopped down from the bench and cautiously pushed the door open.

A short, balding gentleman with spectacles was sitting behind a counter. "Can I help you?" He smiled.

"Yes," said Sammie. "I'm looking for information about an undeveloped area in town, made up of field and woodland." She spelled out its official coordinates with care. "Fifty-five-twenty-eight to fifty-five-fifty Split Road. Do you have any records about it?"

The man looked a little surprised. Adults often did when Sammie started to talk. He rolled back his chair. "Let me see what we've got."

He rose and rummaged through a large gray filing cabinet. "What do you want to know?"

Sammie frowned. "I just think something might be happening to it."

After a few minutes, he pulled out a manila folder. "Aha. I knew it had to be in here somewhere." He leafed through.

Then he peered over the counter at her. "How did you know about this? You're quite a young thing to be paying attention to land sales and development."

Sammie flushed. "I just— I— I live nearby." He looked at her kindly, and his manner warmed her. She decided to trust him. Maybe he could help. "My friend Bram and I are doing a scientific project about the wildlife there. And I saw flagging on the trees. I don't want anything built on that land. It's my favorite place in the world."

"I see," said the man. He rubbed his chin. Then he bent his head again over the file.

"The parcel belongs to the city," he said. "They've just bought the house flanking it, too. And they're selling the whole lot. Says here the primary likely buyer is called Winston Builders."

"Winston Builders," Sammie repeated, going cold with fear and rage. That sounded bad.

"Huh," he said. "Odd. Usually there's more than one bid for a property like this."

"What's a bid?" Sammie asked.

"It's a request to buy the land, stating how much money

they're willing to pay," said the clerk. "More bids must be coming."

"How . . . how does the city decide who gets the property?"

"Usually it goes to the highest bid. But bidders submit plans, too, so the city can decide if they fit in with our development goals."

"Well, they don't!" exclaimed Sammie. "The city shouldn't sell it!"

"Well, dear, I'm afraid there may not be much that can be done. Looks like it was put up for sale a few years ago, too, but I guess no one wanted it then. Unless someone else puts in a bid, Winston Builders will buy it." He looked down with a gentle smile. "It's hard when things change. I know."

"It's worse than just change!" insisted Sammie. "Winghaven has more nature and animals than you can imagine. Muskrats and pileated woodpeckers and hydras, and blackberries and mice and milk snakes and antlions and monarch butterflies—they're the most important of all—and they need milkweed so that they can breed! They're in trouble and they need our help!"

The man stared at her, wonder behind his wire-rimmed glasses. "You're one smart little kid," he said. "You know, there's normally a public hearing when land is sold. This one's next Friday at five p.m. in the Community Room."

Just then Sammie heard her mother's voice, echoing in conversation against the hallway's stone walls.

"Thank you very much," she said hastily. "I have to go." She hurried out.

Her mother was on her cell phone. Sammie could just hear the tinny voice of the person on the other end of the line.

"Every year. Oh, thank goodness," said her mother.

Tinny voices again.

"I'd like a copy of the vaccination records. Oh, your vet's number? Yes, I'll wait."

Her mother covered the phone with one hand when she saw Sammie.

"They moved to a new house here in town," she said in a low voice. She seemed too preoccupied to bother about where Sammie had been. "Looks like that dog was vaccinated, thank heavens."

She uncovered the phone. "Go ahead." Soon she was scribbling in her datebook.

Sammie plunked onto a hall bench. Her wrist hurt less with the news. As she waited for her mother to finish her phone calls, her mind churned on what she had discovered.

36
THE SYMPOSIUM

Sammie felt very small.

She stood in the Audubon Society doorway, her arms full of posters. Her dad was behind her, carrying a canvas bag of specimens.

Sammie's mom was at work, it being Saturday morning. Maybe she would arrive before the symposium ended, Sammie thought without much hope.

Could her mom be too angry about Winghaven to come see Sammie's project? Or did she just feel like she couldn't miss yet another day of work this week?

The room looked larger and more intimidating than during the Christmas Bird Count. It was full of people—all adults—in long aisles created by the big wooden tables where they were setting up their work. When the public would be welcomed a half hour from now, Sammie couldn't imagine how packed it would be.

Just then Jean Sand appeared from among the aisles like a rabbit from a hole. "Sammie!" Her weathered face lit in a smile. "Right this way, my young friend. I've got a table all ready for you."

She extended a hand. "You must be Sammie's dad. I'm Jean Sand."

"Dave." Sammie's dad beamed. "A pleasure."

They followed her. Jean's presence made Sammie feel more comfortable. But as swiftly as she'd appeared, she was gone, her face brightening again to see another new arrival at the main door.

Sammie stared at the empty wooden table. Right now, she felt like a little kid—not a scientist. Where was Bram? There wasn't much time before the symposium started.

"Be right back," said her dad, heading for the bathroom.

Slowly, Sammie began to unpack the materials she and Bram had worked so hard to make.

As she started setting up, a bit of confidence came back to her. The materials were so familiar—the rough poster-board against her hands; the clear plastic specimen cases; the faint crinkle of leaves as she carefully opened a few herbarium pages.

She inspected the table, deciding how to lay out their project. She placed the specimens in front, each with a label describing where and when it had been found. Delicately she fingered the box where she'd stretched the milk snake's shed skin, its transparent scales sparkling in the overhead lights.

One poster showed the Field's plant life, complete with Sammie's pressed flowers. Another, photos and drawings of birds. A third, mammals. Right in the middle, Bram had printed one of his favorite photos: the Pond's muskrat carving its way through the water.

The huge monarch poster—their pièce de résistance—stretched across the back, bright with colors, the graphs neatly framed, the glossy orange-and-black wings of adult monarchs and the clown-like stripes of the caterpillars shining in Bram's photos.

By comparing their plot with other sites from the Monarch Larva Monitoring Project, Sammie and Bram had discovered that Winghaven had more monarchs than anywhere else as far north as New England. They'd found as many monarch caterpillars as the MLMP scientists had at their main Minnesota site—about one per plant. And their plot was chock-full of milkweed, too. Winghaven really was perfect for monarchs.

If only she had gotten better photos of the tire tracks and flagging around the Field. A small side display she'd made last night showed Robert's single woodland photo with a description of the threat to Winghaven, but it was overshadowed by the other posters. It would have to do— she could point people to it and describe what she'd learned.

She kept a keen eye on the door. Each time it opened, her heart lifted with hope and then fell. Then another kid walked in—but it wasn't Bram.

Under the archway of the door stood Robert. He looked a little lost, clutching his project in his arms. He wore a stiff, collared shirt and tie and had gelled his hair back like a salesman. He was alone, without his dad or anyone else.

Jean Sand, though, hurried to welcome him. Sammie strained her ears, but she couldn't hear what Jean said over the hum of voices in the room. In consternation she watched as Jean brought Robert straight toward her.

"I've got a spot for you right next to your schoolmates, Robert." Jean gestured to the next table down from Sammie's and beamed, clearly unaware of the tension between the two kids. "How great to have all of you here together. It's the first year we've had a youth division. You're our pioneers. Where's Bram, Sammie?"

"He'll be here soon," Sammie replied a little woodenly.

She sure hoped he would. What if his plane had gotten delayed? She couldn't bear being at the symposium with Robert instead of Bram.

Jean vanished again in a bounding stride, as hare-like as ever. Robert and Sammie were left to stare at each other.

"Hi," said Sammie.

"Hi." An awkward silence.

To Sammie's immense relief, her dad returned. "Need any help here, Sammie? Oh, hi there." He glanced between the two of them, seeming to pick up what Jean hadn't. "Is this a classmate of yours, Sammie?"

"This is Robert, Dad. He . . . he's got a project here, too."

"Aha. Good for you, young man."

"Sure," said Robert, frowning. "Anyway, I've got to set up my project."

"Okay," said Sammie. And Robert turned away.

The main doors opened again, and a brown-haired, spectacled, slim shape stepped in at last.

"Bram!" She jumped up and down and waved to beckon him over.

She saw his head turn, slow as a turtle, searching. He spotted her. Behind him, his parents stepped in.

And then—Sammie caught her breath.

Her mom was here, too.

Bram rushed over with the last bag of materials. "I'm so sorry we're late," he said, putting it down. He hardly looked at Sammie. "Here, let me set these up quick."

While Bram fiddled with the layout of a few last photographs he'd brought, making sure each was angled just so, the four adults began reading through the posters.

"Bram, these photos," said Vicky. "They're gorgeous. You've improved so much since the last time I saw your pictures. And, Sammie, the descriptions! So articulate."

Sammie's dad reached over and gave her shoulder a squeeze. "That's my girl," he said. "You always do great."

"It's quite extraordinary, the work you two have done," added Bram's dad. "Professional quality."

The praise from a real working scientist felt good—but right now, Sammie's attention was on her mom.

Susan was studying the posters, picking up each box of specimens, reading each word. Her forehead was knitted. It took a long time before she finally looked up.

She had a funny look on her face, one Sammie hadn't seen before.

"You did all these drawings?"

Sammie nodded. "Yeah. And the writing is mostly mine." She couldn't meet her mom's eyes. So much of this she'd done without her mom's approval and then topped that off by trespassing and getting bitten by a dog. She spoke fast. "The herbarium pages—the dried plants—those are mine, too. Bram did the photos and a lot of the calculations."

Glancing up, Sammie realized her mom had tears in her eyes, and she wasn't smiling.

Just then Jean Sand's voice cut through the room's hubbub. "Five minutes until we open the doors to the public!"

37

BAD NEWS

Vicky spoke. **"Why don't we leave you kids alone to** make sure you have everything the way you want? Susan and Dave, let's look around before the crowd thickens."

"Sounds like a great idea," said Sammie's dad. No one else had noticed Sammie's mom's tears.

The adults walked away. Sammie's eyes anxiously followed her mom, but then she pulled her attention back. Now she could finally talk to Bram. She looked at him—and immediately realized something was wrong.

Red splotches stained Bram's normally pale cheeks. He was breathing fast. He looked back at Sammie, and then his eyes dropped away.

"Bram," she faltered, "what's the matter?"

Bram tapped a foot anxiously up and down.

"I have some bad news," he said. "I have to tell you now. I won't be able to focus today otherwise."

Sammie's heart gave a little clench, like a mouse flinching into a hole. Bram so seldom admitted he was worried about anything.

He took a deep breath and dared to glance at her. "My . . . my dad's getting a new job."

"Oh." Sammie couldn't find it in herself to say anything more. Bram seemed to take forever to start talking again.

"He has a temporary professorship here, and we thought he might get a permanent spot," said Bram. "For months, though, he's been waiting to find out about the job he really wanted. When we left Seattle, the university didn't have space for another physics professor. But . . ." Bram swallowed. "But now they do."

"Oh no," blurted Sammie.

"So we're moving back. At the end of the school year."

"No!"

Sammie's voice shook. She didn't want to cry in the middle of the Audubon center.

"I've been stressed about this the whole school year," said Bram. "That's why we took this trip—for my dad's final interview. Plus, my mom wanted me to visit the school I'd applied to, and I had to audition for the orchestra. Then they offered him the job."

A flash of anger seemed to rescue Sammie from her sadness. No wonder Bram had so often seemed preoccupied and distant. "Why didn't you *tell* me?" she burst out.

"I just couldn't!" yelped Bram. "I didn't want to upset you. I thought it might not happen, and then you'd be worked up for nothing. And besides, my dad was supposed to keep it secret."

"I thought you *wanted* to go back to Seattle," Sammie said accusingly. "Now's your chance! Shouldn't you be glad?"

"That's what my parents thought, too," said Bram. "But leave Winghaven, and not get to spend time with you anymore? And not get to count monarchs again next summer?"

Sammie stared up at the fluorescent lights, fighting tears. "Winghaven might not even be there by then," she said. "I found out at city hall that Winston Builders is buying the land. There's supposed to be a public hearing on Friday, but it hasn't been announced in the paper or anywhere. No one's going to try to stop the sale if they don't even know about it."

"That's awful." Bram scrunched his brow. He looked like he was about to cry, too. "We have to do everything we can before then to make people pay attention. Our project has got to show people today how much Winghaven matters."

"I hope it can," she said in a choked voice. "Nothing else has gone right."

"You know, Sammie—" Bram reached out and squeezed her hand. Despite the glisten in his own eyes, he was trying to reassure her. "My photos finally feel important, like they mean something. Until I met you, I never thought of using them for a project like this. And I never thought I'd like it better out here than Seattle—but I do."

Sammie bit her lip. "You really mean that?"

"Swear to God and hope to die," said Bram, his voice choking up. "You're my best friend ever, Sammie."

Sammie fumbled for something to say.

At that moment Jean Sand's voice broke in again. "Doors opening to the public!"

For Sammie, the morning she'd looked forward to for so long passed in a haze. She couldn't keep her mind off Bram's news. People stopped by their project and asked them questions. Some of them were scientists. Sammie answered mechanically as they examined the drawings and sketches and pressed plants and turned specimens over in their hands.

She and Bram tried to point out, to each visitor, the small display on the side that explained Winghaven's trouble. They wanted to reach as many people as they could.

"The hearing is this Friday," she heard Bram say again and again. "Please come!"

Just a few feet away from them, she was dimly aware of Robert also describing his work and talking to people. But she didn't have the heart to look at him or his project. She had enough on her mind.

As the morning wore on, Jean Sand came over for the first time since the kids had arrived.

"I finally have time to look at your projects!" she said. "I've heard so many good things already from the people who've come over to talk with you."

Jean glanced at their table and Robert's. "I know both of you, but this young man is new to me. Robert, why don't you give us a tour of your work."

Surprise seemed to cross Robert's face at being picked first. He glanced at Sammie and Bram, ran a nervous hand over his gel-slicked hair, and nodded.

Sammie and Bram drifted to Jean's side.

His project was titled *Hunting, Wilderness, and Conservation.*

Robert's photos weren't as clear and crisp and striking as Bram's. Where Bram's birds and animals seemed to leap off the page, complemented by the colors and shapes of the nature around them, Robert's photos were duller, the animals less naturally composed against their landscapes. Still, he'd worked hard. He'd even captured some animals Sammie had never seen. A stoat, whiskery and alert with gleaming eyes. And amazingly, a bobcat, only barely visible as it escaped into woodland brush.

Robert's posters explained that good hunters observe and take responsibility for nature.

"If hunters killed too many animals, there wouldn't be

any left to hunt, so we always follow the rules," Robert said. "Hunters know how to be patient and silent. We know how to track animals' trails and learn their habits. Naturalists could learn a lot if they'd just talk to hunters."

"His project's actually pretty good," whispered Bram to Sammie, a bit too loudly.

Robert shot him a glance. Sammie elbowed Bram sharply.

Jean spoke smoothly into the gap. "You're absolutely right, Robert. I'm so pleased you've joined us today to show people that there's more than one healthy way to engage with nature."

Again Robert looked surprised. Then he shot a triumphant glance at Sammie. She looked uncomfortably at her shoes.

At last Jean turned to Sammie and Bram. She smiled and squeezed each of their shoulders. "All right, then, my two young naturalists. Let's have a look at this project I've heard so much about."

Sammie's heart was hammering with anxiety. Jean was important. If they could convince her that Winghaven needed to be saved, she might really be able to help. Sammie knew the Audubon Society bought land to protect birds. Now she was extra glad that in addition to the monarch material, they'd created one large poster about birds, listing all the species they'd ever seen in Winghaven and displaying

Sammie's drawings of ovenbirds and warblers and wood-cocks and snipes, plus Bram's spectacular photos of hawks, like the harrier over the summer grasses and the merlin zinging through the winter sky.

Jean took a long time browsing their project. Then she bent to Sammie's small warning placard.

She gave a long sigh.

"I thought that land had been sold long ago," she said. "I remember when it came on the market. I was relieved when we found out from Pete that they'd removed it."

Sammie leaped in. "But now they've put it up for sale again!" she exclaimed. "Couldn't the Audubon Society buy the land instead? There's a hearing at city hall this Friday afternoon. Please, Jean—it'd be the very best place to spend your land-purchase fund, we know it would!" She was babbling now, waving her hands at their posters, but she didn't care. "Just look at all these birds we've seen. And the animals we spotted and that Robert did, too. And how many monarchs we counted. We just can't let it be destroyed. Please help, Jean, please."

There was a long, long silence as Jean gazed at their project. Her keen, weathered face looked sad, the first time Sammie had seen it that way. "Our fund is depleted after all these years of a bad economy. We just don't have the money for such a valuable expanse of land. I wish we did." She sighed. "I'm not sure why the city didn't announce this—if we'd known sooner, maybe we could've held a fundraiser, but it's too late now."

Sammie, Bram, and even Robert stood silently, taking in Jean's words. All their work and hopes were coming to nothing.

"I'll come to the hearing, but I don't think there's much more we can do."

38

THE DARK NiGHT
OF THE SOUL

The symposium was drawing to its close. As it did, a young woman stepped from the dwindling crowd.

"I'd like a photo of you kids, please," she said in a clipped voice.

She had a great mane of very curly long black hair, a square jaw, and a long face. Her nose was rounded, and her large black eyes were fringed by long dark lashes. Around her neck she wore a badge that read PRESS.

"Who are you?" said Sammie.

The young woman didn't answer. Instead, she gripped Robert firmly by the shoulder and propelled him to stand next to Sammie and Bram. "Here, let's get all of you in one shot."

"Who are you?" echoed Robert, scowling.

"Don't move," said the photographer firmly, lifting a large camera to her eyes. Her voice had a ring of authority.

Bram, Sammie, and Robert froze automatically in place. The shutter clicked.

"One more. Stand a little sideways so your projects show."

She had, Sammie thought, a face like a show horse. But she looked more determined than glamorous.

The flash went off.

"I'm taking a few photos for the *Herald*," said the young woman. At their blank expressions, she said, "I'm a reporter. Thanks." And she turned and began walking away.

The three kids blinked at her retreating shape. Then Robert looked at Sammie. "Hey, aren't you being kind of an idiot?" he said. "She's a reporter. *She* could let people know what's happening to Winghaven."

For a second Sammie stared at him, surprised and confused. She couldn't tell if Robert was trying to be a jerk or—for the second time—actually trying to help. The word *Winghaven* sounded so strange coming from him. Then she woke up to the meaning of his words.

She chased after the reporter and clutched her sleeve. "Wait," Sammie said. "Don't you . . . don't you want to look at our project?"

The woman seemed annoyed. "I'm here to write about science," she said. "Not a science fair project."

"But it *is* science. And it's really important."

"I'm sure it is, sweetie." The reporter smiled tightly. "Right now I'm on a deadline. Here's my card. Your picture will be in the paper on Monday." Then she pulled her sleeve free and headed out.

That night, Sammie stared up into the dark.

Above her head, the fluorescent stars she'd stuck to her bedroom ceiling in the shapes of constellations had already begun to fade. They were always brightest when she first turned out the light. Trying to make herself tired, she traced the shape of Orion with her eyes, then the Big Dipper. Then Scorpio.

It was no use. She was worrying about too many things.

Bram leaving as soon as the school year ended. Her mom not saying anything about their project. Pete gone to Washington. Winghaven about to be sold.

Sammie kept remembering the image of the little butterfly she and Bram had raised, flying bravely but maybe hopelessly away from them, like Winghaven itself.

The disappointment from Jean Sand followed by the humiliation from the unfriendly reporter played over and over in her head.

Remembering upset Sammie all over again. She threw back the covers and got out of bed.

Softly, in her bare feet and pajamas, she opened her

bedroom door. Careful not to step on the creaking parts of the wood, she crept up the stairs to her Science Room.

She didn't turn on the light. She just stood silently in the darkness.

Around her she could smell the scent of the wooden beams, mixed with the musty smell of nests and feathers and insect husks. She could even pick out the cold metallic scent of rocks she had collected.

As her eyes adjusted, the dark shapes of the shelves, her desk, her familiar things met her gaze. The microscope stood silhouetted by the paler window like a long-necked bird. The symposium posters leaned in the corner. On the shelves rested her specimens, just visible in the window's faint light.

She ran her hand over the smooth contour of a deer bone, then touched the whorl of a snail shell. She fingered the rough twigs of a robin's nest. She'd learned she wasn't supposed to have that, since collecting nests is illegal, but she'd had this one forever and just couldn't bring herself to give it up. She lifted it to her nose to breathe in the aroma of dried leaves and moss and mud.

Everything ended. Nothing could stay. Even her specimens were the signs of animals that had died or flown south—or tried, possibly never to return.

Beyond the window, a prickle of stars burned in a black

sky. She gazed out at them and sighed, tears aching at the back of her eyes.

Again in her mind's eye she saw the reporter walk away.

A clench of anger tightened Sammie's throat.

On the desk beside the microscope, the reporter's card lay crumpled, a pale knot in the dark where Sammie had flung it when she got home.

She picked it up and slowly flattened it onto the desk. Then she turned on the light. A golden glow spilled its diffuse sphere into the small room. REBA R. THOMAS the card read. THE HERALD, 30 FRONT STREET, WESTHAM. REBAR@THEHERALD.COM.

Sammie thought about Bram, and Pete, and Winghaven with all its creatures.

All along, Winghaven had held and protected her. Now it was in trouble. She had to try to give back what it had given her.

She sat down, opened her school laptop, and began to write.

FROM: sammietabithasmith@gmail.com

TO: rebar@theherald.com

SUBJECT: City's secret development plans along Split Road

Dear Reba,

You need to know something important. The big field and woodland by Split Road are about to get sold. We think the city is keeping it secret. The city calls the lot 5528–5550 Split Road. But my science partner Bram and I call it Winghaven. And while Winghaven looks like empty land, it isn't empty at all. We study nature there every afternoon while our parents are still at work, and it's the one place in the world where we never feel lonely.

Have you ever seen an orange-and-black butterfly as big as a jam jar lid? It's the monarch butterfly, the world's most famous. Monarchs migrate thousands of miles each year from Mexico. But their numbers are falling because there are so few grasslands left. Their caterpillars only eat milkweed leaves. In Winghaven, we have thousands of milkweeds—and hundreds of monarch caterpillars. At the Audubon Society Christmas Bird Count, we counted more birds at Winghaven than anywhere else in the city. We were invited to present our findings at the Audubon Society Science Symposium this spring.

Winghaven is in trouble. A developer, Winston Builders,

wants to build there. The public hearing Friday should have been announced in the paper, but Bram and I couldn't find anything. The city is supposed to get bids from anyone who wants to buy the land, but only Winston Builders seems to know about it. They put in the only bid. The city didn't even put up a sign.

Don't you think you could write a story? We need to protect the nature we have left. For kids like me and Bram to learn about it. For birds and mammals. For the monarch butterfly, which needs our help.

Please.

Sincerely,
Samantha Tabitha Smith, age 11

---

attachments:

39

LAST CHANCES

When Sammie went down to breakfast the next morning, she found her mom sitting alone. Her mom patted the seat of a kitchen chair beside her, and Sammie sat down. Her mom looked so serious. Was she finally going to say something about the project? Was she still angry? Did she know about Bram?

Suddenly she found herself blurting out, "I'm so sorry I let you down, Mom. I know I scared you and hid the truth. I . . . I just didn't know what to do. Losing Winghaven would feel like losing everything." Her voice cracked, and she found the words hard to say. "But I don't want to be someone who disappoints you. I can't seem to do anything but let you down."

"Oh, Sammie," said her mom. Her eyes were suspiciously bright. "It's not like that at all. You are the most amazing person I know."

Sammie blinked. She couldn't meet her mom's gaze.

"Your project was so beautiful," her mom said. "I didn't realize what an impressive thing you could make out of a bit of empty land like that."

"I . . . I thought you didn't like it. That you were still mad at me for going there alone and getting bitten."

"I loved your project. It helped me realize that we've been letting you down, too, Sammie," said her mom. "You scared us so much with that dog, but we're also to blame. We've been so stressed, we haven't made time to help you grow and make your ideas come to life. You've been doing it all alone—until Bram, that is. And . . . I'm sorry."

Her mom opened her arms, and Sammie reached for her embrace. Tears began running freely from the corners of her eyes.

"I talked with your dad. We've decided we can get by without my tutoring. We'll have more time to be with you, at least on the weekends. Maybe you can take me to Winghaven. I'd like to see it through your eyes."

Her mom's warm hug set Sammie's sobs free. "If it's still there," she cried, buried in her mom's arms. "They're going to tear it down to build something. And Bram is going back to Seattle. Everything has gone wrong."

"Oh, Sammie. I am so sorry." Her mom held her close, and Sammie let herself cry until she was exhausted.

At Winghaven the next day, Bram was at his boulder as usual. But he was frowning. Wordlessly he handed Sammie a copy of the local newspaper.

Sammie couldn't believe it. Reba had written about them! The article sprawled across the front page. A huge photo of Sammie, Bram, and Robert at the symposium took up the center of the paper. The headline read SCIENCE WHIZ KIDS BLAZE A TRAIL.

"Huh," said Sammie. "We're not whiz kids. That's dumb. And what does Robert have to do with anything?"

"Read the rest," said Bram.

"Three lonely latchkey kids teach themselves about the environment in a saga of determination," Sammie read the headline subtitle aloud. Why wasn't she writing about Winghaven?

"*'Latchkey'*?" she said in indignation. "She shouldn't call me names. Lots of kids are like me!"

"Yeah, who calls anyone that anymore? She shouldn't have said it," Bram said. "And it's not even true about me!"

Reba made them sound pathetic and young, like they were just filling empty afternoons. She'd talked to Jean Sand to find out more about them but hadn't bothered to actually call Sammie, Bram, or Robert themselves. Sammie opened the paper to read the rest of the article. "There are some paragraphs about the developers way down here," she said.

The interior headline subtitle looked more promising: *Grassland haven for birds, butterflies up for development.*

As they'd learned, the city had put the lot up for sale four years earlier. Because the economy hadn't been good, no one had wanted to buy it. Sammie understood that. That was right when her dad hadn't been able to keep his new company going.

The city had done all the notifications when they'd first decided to sell. The lot had been advertised in the paper, just as it was supposed to be. But the announcement had been written in complex legal language, and most residents of the area hadn't noticed, especially since no one bought it right away.

"Winston Builders waited for their moment. When they finally decided it would be economically feasible to buy the property, they went quietly to city hall to ask the city to put it back up for sale and to bid before anyone else," Bram read aloud. *"The city administration wanted to get the property transferred to Winston Builders quickly and without too much competition. Winston Builders was a contributor to Mayor Dan Brody's campaign."*

"That's just wrong!" exclaimed Sammie. "It's good that Reba explained it."

"But look at *this*. She called the mayor and let him put his two cents in." Bram read:

"'The sale of this lot will bring in needed revenue to the city at

a difficult time in our finances,' said Mayor Brody. 'It might be a nice place for some kids to play, but voters understand we have to pay for schools for everyone.'"

Sammie was momentarily speechless. "That . . . that . . ."

"Rotten crook." Bram finished her sentence for her. "My mom said some parents were complaining that the schools aren't getting repaired, but city hall's slated for an upgrade. She bets they're going to use the money for fancy new offices."

"And here, Reba interviewed Winston Builders! *'We believe our complex will be good for the city economy. Local companies will be able to grow.'* How could Reba put that in her article?"

"She does say Split Road might not be able to handle all the new traffic," said Bram.

"No one's going to care about that," said Sammie mournfully. How could the dreams of a couple of kids—and the needs of a fragile, voiceless threatened butterfly—stop powerful people who were promising money and growth for the town?

Despite all Sammie's hopes, Reba's article didn't seem like it would help Winghaven at all.

40
THE HEARING

"Looks like I'll have to park down the street." Vicky pulled up to city hall and circled once around its full parking lot. "You two hop out. I'll meet you there."

Clutching a rolled copy of the *Herald* with their article and a clipboard holding a sheet of paper, Sammie jumped out and raced after Bram. They dodged a few pedestrians, bounded up the steps, and pushed open the building's heavy glass doors. "Community Room," said Bram, gesturing to an arrow pointing down the stairs.

They strode purposefully into a tiled hallway. The Community Room was located right next to city hall's back entrance. People were entering and walking straight into the room.

"Whoa," whispered Bram to Sammie.

The room was crammed with people. Most chairs were already taken. Some people had decided to stand at the back. Bram headed for some open seats at the front.

Before she could follow, Sammie heard a voice from behind her.

"Hi, Sammie," said Reba cheerfully.

She frowned. "Hi, Reba. Why didn't you email me back?"

"I already had plenty of information," said Reba breezily. "And the editors had a spot for it right on the front page." She cast a satisfied look around the room.

"But you hardly wrote about Winghaven!" burst out Sammie, losing her temper. "You just wrote about me and Bram and Robert—not even the monarchs!"

Reba laughed, a throaty chuckle. "Did I need to?" She gestured at the crowd. "Didn't you check online? My story went viral."

Sammie was left speechless.

"What you don't understand is that you kids *are* the story of Winghaven," Reba went on. "Journalists have to entertain people, keep 'em reading. By the middle of the article, they're caught up in your story. They want you to succeed. Then Winghaven gets threatened, and their emotions are already all worked up. I think I managed it pretty well, all told."

Sammie looked around the room. Among the throng of unfamiliar people, she recognized some faces. Her sixth-grade teacher was here. And she could see a person or two that she'd talked to at the Audubon symposium. She didn't see Jean Sand anywhere, though.

Then from behind her, she heard another familiar voice.

"Hey, Sammie."

Sammie startled. "Robert!" she exclaimed. "You came!"

"Of course I did." He turned. "This is my dad."

A burly man had entered behind Robert. He had a red face with a smooth bald pate and tufts of hair that stuck out around his ears. He didn't smile. He did, though, hold out a large red hand to shake Sammie's.

"Robert told me about what you and your friend are doing to save that woodland," he said. "Your folks must be proud."

Sammie flushed scarlet. "Thanks."

"Sure," he said. "I'll go find a seat."

From behind him, Reba shot Sammie a look that said, "I told you so." Then she slunk away to the room's back corner, unfolding her notebook as she went.

Sammie started to follow Bram.

"Hey, wait," said Robert.

Sammie looked at him. After everything that had happened, she wasn't sure what to feel about Robert anymore.

"Uh . . ." He hesitated. Finally he went on, "I never said congratulations for your symposium project. It was really good."

"So was yours," she said cautiously. "Congratulations."

"Nah." He shrugged. "I hope they don't build on Winghaven."

"Same here," she said. Then she added shyly, "I'm . . . I'm also sorry for what I said about your dad. It was nice of you both to come today."

Robert cleared his throat and looked off to the side of the room. "You know, my dad's never home in the afternoons, either."

Was he trying to be nice or teasing her about the latchkey kid thing?

"I didn't realize you were kind of like me, spending a lot of time on your own." He stuck his hands in his pockets. "I thought you and your parents were, like, perfect and you had everything you wanted."

Sammie shook her head silently.

"And, um . . . well, since I live right by there, I thought maybe we could hang out at Winghaven sometime. You know, if they don't build on it."

She blinked at him. All of a sudden he looked up, grinned at her, and sauntered off. "See ya later."

For the first time in Sammie's life, Robert had been nothing but nice to her. She realized in shock that he'd left her with a warm feeling creeping slowly up from her toes.

"Please take your seats," said a man into a microphone at the front podium. "We're about ready to start."

Sammie hurried to join Bram at the front. Bram's mom had come in and was sitting beside him. Sammie hoped her own parents would arrive soon. They'd promised but would be late.

A square-chested man in a crisp suit took the podium mic. Sammie recognized him from his photo in the newspaper. He had a sweep of black hair neatly kept in place with gel and was wearing a bright red tie.

"Welcome, everyone," said Mayor Brody. "It seems there's a surprising amount of interest in our land-parcel sale." Was that sarcasm in his voice? "I hope you'll be impressed with what we have planned."

Sammie and Bram exchanged glances. Bram rolled his eyes.

The mayor flicked open a presentation on the big screen.

"We've had the good fortune to have Winston Builders put forward a strong proposal for its development. I'll walk you through the plans and how they'll help the city."

"How come the mayor's speaking for Winston Builders?" whispered Bram, leaning to Sammie's ear. "Shouldn't they have to present their own proposal?"

The mayor started with a droningly boring history of the city's development, followed by a long presentation of the city's finances. By the time he got back to Winghaven, Sammie was about ready to fall asleep.

She straightened immediately, though, when he began showing maps.

They were the shape of Winghaven but couldn't have been more different from Sammie's careful drawings of trees and grass and path and pond. Just a slim strip of trees would divide Sammie and Bram's neighborhood from a huge new complex. All the grassland would become a large shopping center. A new ramp to the highway cut through the pines. And the Pond? Drained completely for parking.

Sammie stared horrified while Mayor Brody gushed about how convenient the new highway ramp would be. Then he switched slides to a chart with so many entries, they were too small to read—except one. At the top of the slide was the sum of money Winston Builders would pay. Almost three million dollars.

"You can see here exactly how the money's going to help our town." The mayor waved a vague hand at the tiny little figures. "We'll divide the money up among these departments. You can see it's obviously going to make a huge difference."

He hurriedly changed slides.

A dissatisfied murmur ran through the audience. A few hands shot up.

"Of course all this is preliminary—it could change!" said the mayor loudly. "Hold your questions for now. Let's get Mr. Winston up here."

A short, redheaded man with a bristly mustache took the podium. "How's everybody doing?" he said in a bluff, breezy voice, looking out with a big smile.

Sammie disliked him instantly.

"Thanks, Mayor Brody, for that great description of our project!" he gushed. "Couldn't be a better town for it. We think it'll be fabulous. You all live in a great spot, so much potential!"

The audience was silent. Beside Sammie, Bram was scowling.

"We've already had unexpected numbers of people visiting our new mall on Split Road," Mr. Winston went on. "This town is hungry to get bigger. Our complex will make this place a real destination."

Sammie scribbled furiously, editing the sheet of paper on her clipboard.

"The mayor's covered the details. I'll leave it at that. Thank you."

Bram leaned over again. "This guy's super fake! The mayor's a lot slicker than he is," he murmured. "No wonder the mayor did most of the talking."

"We'll now open for public comment," said Mayor Brody. "Please come to the mic in the center of the room."

41

TEAMWORK

An iron indignation was gathering inside Sammie, hold-ing her up, straightening her spine. She jumped up and walked toward the audience mic in the center of the main aisle. Bram followed.

But other people got there first, including Robert's father.

"I'm John Farnsworth. I was really shocked to find out that land behind our house'll be sold," he said. "I never was told till I saw the article in the paper. And no one asked me or gave me a chance to comment. I don't want a highway ramp behind my place. I chose that house because I like privacy. I don't want no new development, I'll tell you that."

Sammie and Bram grinned at each other. If only everyone in this room felt like Mr. Farnsworth!

The next woman agreed. She said the complex would bring too much traffic to Split Road.

But then the next person stepped forward.

"That land is just empty space," he said. "A bunch of people are just trying to keep their precious backyards to themselves. Bunch of NIMBYs. This money will be good for everyone."

"What's a NIMBY?" whispered Sammie to Bram.

"It means 'Not in My Backyard,'" Bram whispered back. "They're people who don't want something that would be good for everyone else just because they'll have to live next to it."

The man moved away. Sammie and Bram stepped to the mic together. A city hall employee hurried over to lower it to their height.

Sammie firmly clutched her clipboard of notes for what she and Bram planned to say.

Her hands stopped shaking. She was brave. She had survived getting bit by a dog. She had written to Reba. She had faced her mom. She could stand up to the mayor and people like the man who said everyone else was just a NIMBY. She wasn't, she realized, a wild, shy creature like those of Winghaven, fleeing into the underbrush at any sign of threat. She was a scientist and an activist, and it was up to her to stand up for what she loved.

No one had said a word about nature yet. That was her job, and Bram's.

"I'm Samantha Tabitha Smith," she said, "the girl from

the story in the *Herald*. And this is my science partner, Bram Layton."

Applause broke out in the audience, surprising Sammie. She took courage from the sound of support.

"We don't think our town wants to become a bigger city at all. We think people here love the trees and grasses and nature. That's what makes our town special."

Bram leaned forward to the microphone. "What the city did wasn't against the law, but it was still wrong. We may be kids, but we know that when the city reopened the land sale, they should have announced it again to everyone. Then the citizens of our town could have decided what to do."

"Besides, we're here to speak for the animals and plants, not just our backyards," said Sammie. "They can't stand up and talk, so we have to speak for them. We've counted over one hundred and twenty bird species at Winghaven. Monarch butterflies rely on the milkweed that grows there, and they're in big trouble because grasslands are disappearing. We found more monarchs at Winghaven than any other monitored site in our state. If we protect it, we'll breathe cleaner air and have birds at our feeders and butterflies on our flowers. We just have to save Winghaven."

A swell of applause broke out in the audience. Some people even rose for a standing ovation. In the back, Sammie spotted her mom and dad, standing up and clapping, proud smiles on their faces.

After Sammie and Bram sat down, person after person spoke out against the new development. Sammie's heart swelled with satisfaction as her fellow citizens explained why they thought the nature at Winghaven was important.

There were still people waiting for their turn when the mayor leaned forward to the standing microphone on the table in front of him.

"I'm hearing a lot of perspectives about not developing this lot," he said. "I'm surprised, because I think it would be a great thing for the city. But there's a problem, folks. We don't have any other bids for this property. Unless someone else puts out an offer, our hands are tied. We're going to have to sell."

There was a shocked hush.

"Can that be true?" whispered Bram. "Maybe it's just one more lie!"

"Right now the city can't afford to hold on to the lot," the mayor went on. "The budget committee's put its foot down."

"Oh *no*," groaned Sammie. All the hope within her came crashing down to the pit of her stomach, settling into a leaded weight.

Mr. Farnsworth's voice boomed from the crowd.

"Then why'd you even have this hearing? We're going to remember this when the next election comes around!"

A chorus of voices broke out. "Yeah! He said it! Bravo!"

"I'm sorry," said the mayor. He shrugged. "There's just not much I can do."

A small commotion erupted in the line of people still waiting for the microphone. A mild but determined voice was cutting through the disorder. "Excuse me. Can I get through? Pardon me. Gotta get to the front. Sorry. Thanks."

Sammie craned to see what was happening. Then she spotted the person weaving his way toward the microphone. She grabbed Bram's arm. "It's Pete!" she squealed.

It *was* Pete. But he looked different. He wasn't wearing his usual khakis or jeans, or his green vest with all the pockets. His hair wasn't sticking up. He was wearing a neat collared long-sleeved shirt and a pair of gray slacks. He looked like a businessman, proper and formal and buttoned-up, with a serious expression on his normally cheerful face.

She and Bram were half-hidden by the crowd. Pete, however, was used to spotting small animals in the underbrush. He aimed a sudden, birdlike gaze, glittering with bright amusement, at Sammie through all the standing and seated people, and winked.

At that moment Sammie knew he was still the same old Pete she loved.

"He must have seen the article online!" exclaimed Bram. "I can't believe he came all the way here!"

"Sorry to show up at the eleventh hour," said Pete a little breathlessly into the microphone. "It's been a bit of a rush these last couple days."

A hush spread.

"I'm a conservation expert at the Nature Conservancy in Washington, DC," said Pete. "We're specialists in finding projects where land is worthy of saving."

Bram and Sammie clutched one another. A conservation expert. Pete had never fully explained his new job to them.

"This situation was a tough one," Pete went on. "We're very interested in monarch conservation, and I've personally worked with the two fine young scientists who just spoke up, Sammie and Bram. I'm here in great part because of them."

He smiled at them, and Sammie felt her cheeks going red with pleasure and shyness.

"I talked with my boss, but we at the Conservancy don't have much free money lying around right now to work with. I was pretty sure there was nothing I could do. Then I realized we didn't have to do this alone. Jean, give a wave."

Sammie and Bram turned around. There stood Jean with her neat gray ponytail and a tidy blazer at the back of the room. She waved her hand and smiled.

"Jean Sand drove here with me. She's the director of the

regional branch of the Audubon Society. They've been hoping for quite a while to create a nature preserve in this town. They haven't had the resources to do it—but they've been saving up.

"Sammie and Bram's data for the Monarch Larva Monitoring Project shows just how special Winghaven is. Jean and I realized that together, our organizations can afford to buy this land. Her people have been hurrying all day to put a bid together. Jean's ready to submit it right now. We propose a joint Nature Conservancy/Audubon preserve, administered by Jean's team. We'll convert the old house there into a nature center. And the trails and landscape will be open to the whole community."

Applause burst out again. People began to stand, and then more and more of them. The mayor and Mr. Winston sat stunned and scowling at the front of the room, looking like puffed-up balloons that had just been pricked by a pin.

Sammie and Bram jumped to their feet. Pete gave a huge grin and gestured for them to join him at the front of the room. They looked at each other, their faces bright suns with new hope. They gave each other the tightest possible hug. And then they made a beeline for Pete.

42

WiNGHAVEN

Winghaven lay easy and bright in the late June sunlight.
Goldfinches flew in little strands over the glowing grasses,
calling to one another: *"Dit-dit-dit-dit! Dit-dit-dit-dit!"* Higher
still, pilgrim gulls sailed past like always.

The trees were no longer stained with pink and orange
tape. But Winghaven, Sammie knew, would soon change
anyway.

She had biked here extra slowly. Last summer, every day
seemed to last for an eternity, with the monarchs and birds
and sketching and caterpillar counting. Why was time going
so quickly now?

All too soon the entrance had risen in front of her. A neat
footpath entered, no longer an overgrown gap in the shrubs.

A sign marked the entry: WINGHAVEN WILDLIFE
SANCTUARY.

Throughout May and June, Sammie and Bram had met

regularly with the Audubon Society Committee. The two of them had been asked to share their expertise, help decide where paths should lead, and design exhibits for the new nature center planned in the renovated Junkyard House. Much better, thought Sammie, than the shabby clapboard, disorderly yard, and aggressive dog that had so frightened and hurt her.

Sammie and Bram had walked with committee members down the paths. Markers would be pounded along each one: stakes with a colorful shape on top—blue triangles for the Pond path, green squares for the Field path, red circles for the Woodland. The markers reminded Sammie of the construction flagging. These, though, were happy shapes and colors, not threatening ones. Now their place would belong not just to them but to everyone. Its birds and butterflies and snakes and pond would be their secret no longer.

Before leaving again for Washington, DC, Pete had hugged them both tightly. A few days later he'd sent a letter. *I'll be back to visit the university in November,* he wrote. *I'm looking forward to seeing Winghaven as a real preserve when I get back. You and Bram are the true monarchs of Winghaven. Like a king and queen, you are its protectors. I knew you could do it. Congratulations, my brilliant young friends!*

For the first time since she'd met him, Sammie would have Pete all to herself. She could invite him to see her Science

Room if she wanted, like Bram had gotten to have Pete at his house for a whole afternoon. But the idea had lost some of its pleasure.

Sammie sighed and plucked a sprig of sweet fern. Bram hadn't yet arrived. Sammie knew why he was late. This wasn't just any day.

As if her thought had summoned him, she heard his footsteps on the path. She always knew when it was him. He walked more softly than anyone she knew.

She turned.

"Hi."

"Hey."

"I can't stay long," said Bram.

"I know."

They stood looking at each other. For a moment, neither of them knew what to say.

"Did you get the last of your stuff packed?" Sammie finally said.

"Almost," said Bram. "My dad's getting my bike into the trailer right now."

"I wish you didn't have to go."

"I'll send you photos. And you've got to write to me. I'm going to really miss this place."

Sammie nodded. She didn't trust herself not to cry.

"And you, too," added Bram in a quiet voice. Their hands

reached out and clasped together. The touch felt firm and warm and close, like he'd never be gone, and her heart beat warmly and slowly in her chest. They stood hand in hand with all of Winghaven surrounding them.

Far below, the sandy path plunged into the woodland at the end of Winghaven, dark, inscrutable, as if into a hidden future. A clear light played among the tips of the grasses, turning them neon green. The trees made a metallic rustle as a breeze tasted them.

Sammie held Bram's hand tightly. It felt good in hers. Real. Reassuring.

Around them, summer shone and breathed. The perfect silence of nature, not broken but made deeper by the rustle of leaves and the occasional trill of a bird, seemed to gather them up and hold them in a vast lap of wilderness.

"It won't be the same anymore," she said. "So many new people."

"I know," said Bram. "But it's okay. I've got the old Winghaven right here." He patted his camera. "And you've got it here." With the same hand he tapped her notebook, its spiral binding barely sticking out from her pack. "And we've really created something together—become scientists, for real. Collaborators, like you said. And"—he paused, his eyes settling on her—"more than that, too."

Sammie dropped her gaze to the ground.

"Well," he said softly, "I better go. My parents will be waiting."

What was this strange new thing between them? Sammie briefly glanced up but felt too shy to keep his gaze. They stood there at the top of Winghaven, and she felt her cheeks turn pink and hot.

"Bye, Sammie," said Bram softly. He touched her sun-yellow hair. And then she heard his feet pounding off down the path at a run.

Her eyes filled with tears. She stood very still, looking at the sandy ground through their mist, listening to the last sounds recede.

She imagined Bram walking home one last time. She imagined his empty house, his things either in the trailer or already gone in the moving van. She imagined him crossing the country, gazing out the window of his parents' car as Winghaven dropped away behind them. She imagined him writing her letters about Seattle and its nature.

She looked up at last.

All around her, Winghaven lay warm and comfortable and certain, its gold and green flanks softly shining. Together, they had done it. Bram was leaving, but this perfect place would stay, almost the same, innocent and alive. Perhaps it would draw him back, like a migrating monarch. And new companions, both creatures and people, awaited her.

In a tree, she heard the buzzy trill of the early summer bird she'd still never seen, rising, rising, and then breaking off in a little snap, a stick reaching the end of the chain-link fence. Now she'd learned what it was.

She took out her notebook. She wrote the date and the time. *Northern parula,* she wrote, *NOPA*—the right code, just like in Pete's notes. *Song heard on entry path.* Someday she would spot one. So much still waited to be discovered.

She lifted her arms toward the sky and the tree boughs and took a deep, deep breath.

Then she settled her pack more firmly at her waist, lifted her head, set her chin proudly, and set off down the path into Winghaven.

WEATHER: Warm, constant breeze, bright sun
LOCATION: Winghaven
TIME: 10:15 a.m.

In the entrance woods, some animal scat (poop!) on a rock:

Maybe raccoon? 4 in. long, 3/4 in. wide
Contains sunflower seed hulls:
bird feeder near here?

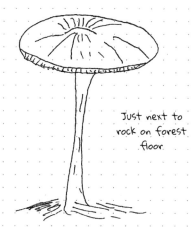

Just next to rock on forest floor.

Many flowers now out as well:

Just inside Winghaven on path:

MOURNING DOVE

yellow

HAWKWEED
Abundant all over Winghaven

Green center

White petals

Also lots of blackberry:

Among the bushes:

CHICKADEES
Singing their "Feebee!" mating whistle

Day of the sun
Day of the breeze
Day of the grass, and the
   plants, and the trees,
Day of the squirrel
Day of the dove
Day of summer
Day to love.

NOTES FOR YOUNG NATURALISTS

(AND THEIR TEACHER/PARENT GUIDES)

Everything that Sammie and Bram do for and with nature in this book, other young people can do, too, with or without the help of parents and teachers. These notes give some background that I used to write this story and also information and books that can help you become a young naturalist.

ON KEEPING A NATURE JOURNAL

Nature journals can create a beautiful record of the wild creatures, plants, and habitats you have observed. They also train you to look at the world deeply.

You don't need to know how to draw, and you don't need to be a good writer. You can learn to do either or both things well enough to make your own journal perfect for you. Anyone—kids or adults—can start keeping a journal at any time.

Some favorite books of mine to help you get started include the following:

Arnosky, Jim. *Drawing from Nature*. Boston: Lothrop, Lee & Shepard, 1987.

Leslie, Clare Walker, and Charles E. Roth. *Keeping a Nature Journal: Discover a Whole New Way of Seeing the World Around You*. North Adams, MA: Storey, 2003.

Mitchell, Andrew. *The Young Naturalist*. Tulsa: EDC Publishing, 2007.

ON CiTiZEN SCiENCE

Citizen scientist projects allow amateurs to help scientists study monarch butterflies. You can count eggs and caterpillars, survey milkweed plants and wildflowers, and monitor ecosystem health, such as by tracking plant and butterfly parasites. Sammie and Bram contribute their data to the Monarch Larva Monitoring Project (https://mlmp.org), a program that has kept track of monarch populations for more than twenty-five years. The MLMP is now jointly run by the University of Wisconsin–Madison Arboretum and the Monarch Joint Venture, an initiative through which citizen scientists can also join other monarch programs (https://monarchjointventure.org).

Nonprofit nature groups near you may organize monarch counts in local meadows. Counting with other people can help you make friends, learn from others, and share the responsibility.

ON RAISING MONARCHS

Students have long enjoyed raising monarchs in captivity to observe the marvel and beauty of their metamorphosis from caterpillar to butterfly. However, young naturalists should know that one study recently done by scientists suggested that monarchs raised indoors may not migrate.

The scientists, a team from the University of Chicago, raised wild-caught caterpillars into butterflies. They then caught wild butterflies to compare the behavior of the two groups. In autumn, they attached all the monarchs—wild and captive—to a pole using a very thin thread and watched the direction the butterflies tried to fly. The wild-caught butterflies usually tried to fly south. However, the ones raised indoors seemed confused and didn't manage to fly in a consistent southward direction.

What Should a Young Naturalist Interested in Monarch Butterflies Do?

The scientist team writes that they still believe that raising butterflies can be an important learning activity. Kids raising monarchs, they explain, have helped create a link between people and nature. In particular, the practice has helped make monarchs the beloved, popular insects so many people are working hard to save, encouraging conservation.

The team believes people can continue to raise monarchs. However, whenever possible, it's better to *collect caterpillars locally* and *raise them outdoors* like Sammie and Bram. That way, the monarchs are most likely to be exposed to the natural environmental cues they need to eventually find their way southward and migrate successfully. And, when rearing monarchs, people can report their results to projects like the MLMP, helping scientists understand important sources of monarch mortality.

ON MONARCH HABITATS

Most of all, monarch butterflies need plants and a good habitat. They need milkweed for their eggs and caterpillars, and they need other wildflowers, whose nectar they feed on. You can help them on their journey.

A pollinator garden at your house or school can create a butterfly habitat. Pollinator gardens are beds of wildflowers and other plants needed by creatures that pollinate plants, including monarchs, bees, moths, other species of butterfly, and even hummingbirds.

Look on the internet or in the library for the best plants for your region, especially native ones. In the northeastern United States, some great native pollinator plants include the following:

Asters (*Symphyotrichum* spp. and others)
Bee balm (*Monarda* spp.)
Butterfly weed (*Asclepias tuberosa*)
Common milkweed (*Asclepias syriaca*)
Coneflowers (*Echinacea* spp.)
Golden Alexander (*Zizia aurea*)
Joe-Pye weed (*Eutrochium purpureum*)
Pearly everlasting (*Anaphalis margaritacea*)

If you're lucky, monarchs or butterflies like the American painted lady or black swallowtail will start laying eggs on your plants, and you can watch the caterpillars grow right in your own backyard.

Pesticides and herbicides can kill insects or make them sick, so it's important not to use chemicals on your pollinator garden. It's also important not to use these chemicals on lawns or vegetable patches, because butterflies, bees, and other important insects can get hurt by them there, too.

ON BIRD-WATCHING

I started my own journey toward becoming a naturalist by learning how to bird-watch. For me, birding became a lifelong practice.

My dad took me bird-watching as a kid and had endless patience when we went outdoors to observe birds. Together, we went on countless Audubon Society field trips, where I learned much of what I know.

The Audubon Society offers field trips all over the United States where you can get started as a young naturalist. In the United Kingdom, where I bird-watched before moving to America, the Royal Society for the Protection of Birds is a similar wonderful organization.

The Audubon Society has run Christmas Bird Counts since the early 1900s. All the data is available for free at the Audubon Society website (www.audubon.org/conservation /science/christmas-bird-count).

ON COLLECTIONS

Making collections of natural objects like Sammie's can be a great learning tool, but nature should be approached with respect and restraint. Collecting nests and feathers, for instance, is forbidden by federal law unless you have a special permit to do so. Many naturalists now believe that when outdoors, one should normally "take only pictures, leave only footsteps." This practice ensures that every being that walks through or lives in nature will have access to the natural objects that belong there. To keep your impact small, take no more than you need.

ACKNOWLEDGMENTS

So many people have helped me with this book.

First, I owe a deep debt to the writing community of my city of Northampton, Massachusetts. You know who you are, even those without individual acknowledgment here. I could not have written this book without the hours spent writing in your company, your cheerleading in person and on social media, your thoughtful responses to my writing, and the inspiration from all that you have written and shared.

Thank you to my elder writing mentors: Susan Stinson, for your mentorship and the writing room where I spent many hours drafting this book; Jane Yolen, steadfast supporter of children's writers everywhere, for befriending, mentoring, cheerleading, and inspiring me; Peter and Jeannine Laird, for your friendship and guidance; Diana Gordon, for shepherding me into the local community.

Thank you to my critique group: Burleigh Mutén, Ann

Desmond, Susan Garrett, and Mary Ellen Kelly—ah, you dear people. You stuck with me through the drafts and years with clever, practical eyes and helped my book incalculably. And thank you to my poetry critique group, Michelle Seaman and Juanita Smart, for reading chapters and giving astute comments and support when I needed it.

Thank you to those who provided technical guidance: Karen Oberhauser of the Monarch Larva Monitoring Project, for fact-checking my monarch life history and letting the MLMP appear in this book; Ted Watt of the Hitchcock Center in Northampton, for conversations on monarchs and local natural history; Stephen Petegorsky, for photography fact-checking; Wayne Feiden, former Northampton planning director, for explaining city land sales; Levi Frye, conservation officer with New Hampshire Fish and Game, for informing me on hunting regulations; the Audubon Society, for a wealth of knowledge and guidance since my childhood; and Cheryl Savageau of Abenaki descent, for discussions on Indigenous understandings of nature. I acknowledge that the natural landscapes in this book are ancestral lands of the Abenaki.

Thank you to Sylvia Liu, Erik Jon Slangerup, and Nicole Collier, publishing-process support buddies. Special thanks go to Sylvia for technical help with the book's illustrations; Joy deBaglio of the Pioneer Valley Writers' Workshop, for space to share this book with others; Carol deSanti, for guidance and warmhearted support on the bumps and benefits of publishing; the Smith College Writers Salon, for a space to vent; my Jacobson Center colleagues, for your support and discussions on writing; and Forbes Library director Lisa Downing, assistant director Molly Moss, and the Forbes Library.

Thank you to my secondary-school teachers Mrs. Hoffa, Mrs. Gaucher, and Mrs. Provencher, who saw a writer in me.

A thousand thank-yous to my editor, Susan Van Metre. You gave this book your time and your astute editing eye, but more importantly, you gave it so much heart. Thank you to Maya Tatsukawa, art editor, for your patient edits; Elly MacKay, for the cover from my wildest dreams; Julia Gaviria and Erin DeWitt, for smart copyedits; the Walker Books US publishing team; and to my agency, Stimola Studios, and its founder Rosemary Stimola, for guidance and comments.

My agent, Allison Hellegers, you deserve a line to yourself. You are a rock star. Thank you for your unfailing support and your deep understanding of the characters of this book.

Thank you to my family: Suzana and Alberto Moreira; Rayane Moreira, Alexei Oblomkov, Sofia, and Damien; Kerry Ryan; and Paul Hacking and Oliver. You are my bedrock.

ABOUT THE AUTHOR

Naila Moreira has loved nature and writing since childhood. Her bird- and nature-watching and her work as a geologist have taken her to the coasts, forests, and grasslands of New England, the Pacific Northwest, Alaska, and Brazil. Through it all, she's kept her pen busy writing about her adventures. A former artist-in-residence at the Shoals Marine Laboratory in Maine, Naila Moreira now teaches at Smith College in Massachusetts, where she lives with her family.